# Spin

## B. John Gully

To Ben & Betsy

Sorry about the busting...
I'll see you at C.U. !!

Marriott Residence Loburn
March 2021
- Brian Gully

3

*Mom, Dad, Toni, & Gizmo, thank you for making our house a home throughout my life.*

# CHAPTER ONE
# MAUDE

After a quiet fit of frustration, I turned my pillow over to its cooler side. For a moment I was relieved of all worry and pain, and brought to a feeling of peace. Not long after, though . . . I sunk back into discomfort. I tried to turn the pillow over again, but it was no use. That coolness had come and gone so fast, and now neither side was more comfortable than the other. I was stuck, sleepless and with a face twitching pathetically from lack of rest.

The top cover of my bed weighed heavy on me, and suddenly I noticed I was coated with sweat underneath it. The heat in the house was turned up high, but the thermostat was all the way downstairs in the kitchen. I thought of getting up to budge open a window and let the crisp fall air in, but assumed that maybe it was best not to move, to stay horizontal, because standing up might have ruined any chances I had at falling asleep.

With my eyes still partially closed, I reached to the night-stand for a glass bottle. It was full of a lavender-scented perfume supposed to affect my brain in such a way that the smell would gently carry me off to sleep. I misted it four times over the pillowcase, soaking the cloth, then lay back down and started to count breaths extending inhales and exhales to five seconds each. I could feel my chest filling with static air and then decompressing upon exhale. Like the lavender, the patterned breathing was also supposed to quiet my brain down, lower my heart rate and send me off into distant dreams, but it was having no effect. The rituals, exercises and aromas I'd taken from bookmarked online forums marked, "non-pharmaceutical cures for insomnia," weren't amounting to anything but further frustration and scorn for the trust I had in the internet's knowledge.

As a breeze blew against the closed window, begging to get inside, I stared up at the white textured ceiling and recalled a sarcastic answer on the forum. It read, "Try a fifth of brown liquor, or maybe even less depending on your tolerance."

I squeezed my eyelids with some force as a cluster of bad thoughts began to make their way into my focus like storm clouds giving the stench of rain. I gave a hard, uninterrupted stare to the wall and the shadows cast on it, and before I knew it I was playing out the events of my days to come and what it would be like to continue to face them with no sleep.

**Bryce**: Mr. Mayor, can you comment on your repeated yawning during the opening of the new south-end recreation center?

**Me**: Well, Bryce I—

**Bryce**: And Mr. Mayor, your constituents are wondering about the ever-growing bags under your eyes. They seem to have tripled in size over the past week, care to comment?

**Me**: Well, you see, a new moisturizer is absolutely—

**Bryce**: And Mr. Mayor, your patience with the mayoral candidates during yesterday's debate seemed exceptionally short. What was that about? Do you believe they are inadequate and wasting your time by running? Namely Councilwoman Iris Acosta-Campos— you realize she is picking up credit with left-leaning voters?

**Me**: Bryce, will you give me a fucking second PLEASE.

*Fuck*, I thought, and turned back over from the imaginary interview. I buried my face deep in the pillow.

A parade of thoughts rapid-fired into my head, tumbling

over one another as if they were racing to be heard. As a result, small fragments of worry bombarded me.

"Drive, coffee, crash, computer, commercial, behind, overdue, lose, drive to, head, bags, lines, eyes, debate, 7-5-no, drive, 5 point, Cristine, lie, lines, eyes, Cristine, head, lie, Maude, school, drive, head, Maude, Maude, crash, sleep, head, Cristine, Maude, Maude, Maude, Maude . . . CRASH."

I blinked hard and jolted at the loud shattering crash — because it was actually real. After a momentary lag, I scurried out of bed and my bare feet stomped against creaky hardwood floors.

I made my way to my bedroom door. When I opened it, Jack the Cat was waiting for me in the hall, and, as if somehow emboldened by my presence, he ran ahead toward the source of the sound. I followed closely behind, stepping down the stairs and looking straight ahead to the front door. I specifically examined the glass of the door, clenching my jaw tightly at first, but relaxing it when I saw that it was all intact.

No one had broken in, at least through the front, and I'd started to gather what was going on based on a small amount of light coming from the kitchen. At the bottom of the stairs I turned my head, knowing exactly what I'd find.

"Maude," I said sternly.

I could see her tiny legs and bare feet underneath the open refrigerator door. Then her knees bent into sight as she picked up a large piece of broken jam-jar and tossed it into the trash.

I stepped forward and pulled the refrigerator door back. When she was spotted, she looked up at me with wide pale blue eyes and light hair that just barely touched the shoulders of her pinstripe pajamas.

"Don't step over here!" she commanded with authority. "You'll hurt your feet."

I gave an appalled grunt and snatched her off the ground before she stepped in any glass, then placed her on the countertop where I prepared to start scolding her. Before I could get a word out, she pointed behind me and called in a brazen voice.

"Jack the Cat!" she said. "Don't let him step in the glass!"

I gave an annoyed sigh and looked down below me, where Jack the Cat was inching toward the debris for a taste of the exposed jam. I put my hand under the pitch-black fur of his belly and lifted him to Maude on the counter. He meowed as she took him in with both arms.

"Good boy," she cooed to him, trying not to look at me.

"What do you think you're doing," I demanded. "It's a school night."

"That's why I'm making peanut-butter and jelly. It's for lunch."

I glanced around the island to see that there were several other groceries laid out on the counter. Maude had apparently gone shopping in our cabinets, and even our freezer, as a package of chicken breasts lay out defrosting. I moved them to the fridge, and then turned back around to take care of Maude.

"It's past midnight. You should be sleeping, not lurking around and raiding the fridge." I'd started to brush the shattered jar into the kitchen dustpan when she responded.

"But you're not sleeping."

"I don't have school tomorrow."

"But you have work."

"Let me see your feet."

I switched on the kitchen light and examined her soles for any tiny cuts that she may not have even registered yet. When I found none, I started to do some wider sweeping. I might have been close to stepping on a shard myself, but I didn't bother get my own shoes; I was secretly enjoying the coldness of the tiles. Had I sidestepped in one wrong direction, I may have crunched my foot on a rogue jagged shard that hid in the corner of the kitchen.

Maude continued to make her argument.

"And your work is way harder than my school. Even Christopher Thompson got almost every question right on our last vocabulary quiz, and he still picks his nose when he thinks no one is looking. But I am looking and I say stop it, because he's almost eight already. And then he still does it the next day!"

"Maude," I cut her off. "It's not your concern what Christopher Thompson gets on his tests, and it's not your business what he does with his boogers."

"But what if he wipes them on me?"

"He doesn't, does he?"

"No, but what if he did?"

"It's time for bed. Your mother is picking you up in the morning and if she sees you haven't slept all night she will not be happy with you."

"How will she be able to tell?"

I ignored her last question, opting to lift her up and carry her off to bed instead. The cat led the way once he saw we were moving, but he continued toward my room once I stopped at Maude's.

"Say goodnight now," I told her.

"Goodnight, Jack the Cat."

When I first moved into my house, I decided I would make sure Maude would be excited to come visit me. I did that by getting not one, but two pets: a cat and a dog to cover all bases. Maude had never been around any pet of her own up to that point, and at the time I wanted more than anything to give her something to be excited about. I told her she could pick any names she wanted for our two new pets. Her choices were Jack, and Jack . . . Jack the Cat and Jack the Dog. I explained to her that I meant she could pick a different name for each one, but her heart was already entirely set, so we had two pets named Jack.

As I set Maude in her bed and helped her under the light blue covers, my eyes started to glass up and I felt myself fading away from her. I was so damn tired and it was even more exhausting to put on the façade of control and capability when I really felt like I could melt into a puddle of goo at any moment.

I hadn't slept more than an hour in four days.

With each passing minute awake it felt as if pressure around my skull was pushing with more weight and force than before.

I'd started to press my fingers into my forehead and rub when Maude spoke. First she continued her full-volume chatter from before, but when I shot her a 'quiet down' look accompanied by a finger, she broke into a whisper.

"Are you going to bed now too?"

"Yes, bug. Everyone's going to sleep, it's late."

"Do you ever stay up all night?"

She'd started to back me into a corner, like she usually could with her questions. And even though I was tired and frustrated, I nearly grinned at the thought of her with an inevitable future as a reporter, the type that doesn't back down from the questions that cut deep. She'd have politicians shaking in their brown leather Oxford's when they were caught in front of her unforgiving stare and notepad. Hell, here she was practicing on me.

Maude demanded truth wherever she went.

"No."

"There was an episode of Spongebob where they kept the Krusty Krab open all night long."

I sighed as I jokingly bopped her on the head with

pillows, then said, "Yeah well, you don't work all night at the Krusty Krab, kid. You hardly watch any T.V., now don't tell me you still want to copy what you see on there."

"No."

I would have gotten up and left, but I could see in her eyes the building blocks to more statements were stacking up. She wasn't finished with me yet.

"One time Mom told her skin doctor that she used to have 'all-nighters' in college."

"Sometimes," I paused, suddenly lagging in my train of thought at the mention of her mother. "Sometimes grown-ups can decide to do that— stay up all night for something. But they almost always wish they didn't, because the next morning they're grumpy, tired, and they don't want to do anything at all."

She'd put on the face again, but I stopped her before she could say anything else by standing up and starting toward the door.

As I walked I said, "And I'll let you know something else, people will frustrate you way more when you're grumpy, especially ones that frustrate you already. That means Christopher Thompson. Get to bed. Trust me; you'll thank me for nagging you."

I said goodnight as I switched her lights off and shut her door, inhaling deeply as the knob clicked shut. I gently pressed my forehead against the wood. The front of my head pulsed in pain, but somehow the flat surface against it was soothing.

I got back to my room to find Jack the Cat waiting in the shape of a ball on my bed, his green eyes visible even in the dark. I fell forward hoping I'd be knocked unconscious the instant my head hit the pillow, but I wasn't so lucky and Jack the Cat scurried away.

*Thanks a lot, cat,* I thought. *Just leave me on my own.*

Against my better judgment, I reached out for my

phone. The light from the screen flashed open and dug its way into my baggy eyelids.

I made the usual rounds on my phone: messages, email, and finally my worst addiction, the numbers. My numbers. That's when I saw . . . fuck. I'm down. I'm down by almost three points . . .

I sat up, my jaw clenching as I frantically swiped through contacts and then opened the name Martin.

*Hey, WTF?! I just checked the new numbers from—*

"Dad?" Maude called as she pushed my door open.

I looked up from my phone and agitation boiled over in my voice, "What are you doing? Did I not just put you in bed?"

She glanced at the phone in my hand and replied, "You're not in bed yet."

"I had to look at something for work," I said sternly, while getting up to carry her back to bed once again. "And you need to stop with the back talk now. It's way too late."

"Were you looking at something about elections?"

She was trying to distract me, get back on my good side since I'd put my foot down on her quips. I wasn't going to fall for it, and I continued straight ahead back to her bedroom.

"I can't sleep," she said.

My heart shuttered and I stopped in the hallway. I looked at Maude expecting to see a reflection of my weathered and tired face in her little eyes that didn't deserve the frustration of a brain that wouldn't turn off. That would have been hard to see. Heartbreaking, even . . . it wasn't what I saw though. She had a big grin on her face like she'd just gotten free ice cream.

"You can't sleep?" I asked sarcastically, thinking to myself that this little brat didn't know the pain of real no sleep.

"Can I sleep in your bed?"

"No."

I avoided looking at her again, for as long as I could.

Not long after that I was getting her settled into my bed, with her own blanket and stuffed animals. I'd limited her to two.

With her next to me I knew the chances of me getting to sleep were completely blown away. But I'd have to at least fake it, otherwise I'd get a call from her teacher the next day about how Maude had fallen asleep face down in art supplies.

I climbed into my bed saying, "School. Mom. Tomorrow . . . Sleep."

She closed her eyes and got quiet, and I breathed a sigh of relief.

"Dad?" She said, not four seconds later. My eyes popped open to see hers met mine. She didn't wait for me to answer before continuing, "Did Jack the Dog go to heaven?"

". . . What?"

"Once he caught that bird in the backyard, and he killed it."

"Maude."

"I yelled at him and told him it was bad, remember? And then you put the bird in a box for me to bury" Her eyes were wide now, her head clearly going a mile a minute in thought. "I didn't give him a treat for like three whole days after that. And then I only gave him half a treat after that until he was sorry, and good."

"Hey," I stopped her gently. "Don't worry so much, okay? Just try to get some sleep."

"Sorry," she responded with disappointment.

After I closed my eyes again, I could feel hers lingering on mine. She spoke one more time, this time quieter, "Do you miss when me, you and Mom all lived together?"

I pretended to be asleep.

"Dad . . . Dad?"

# CHAPTER TWO
# PROGRESSIVE

It wasn't until the early morning, when I'd already noticed birds starting to chirp outside, that my diabolical body decided to grant me a little bit of sleep. Imagine that. I'd gotten so grumpy that I would have given my own circadian rhythm a harsh attitude if it were standing in front of me.

When the doorbell rang in the morning I pried my eyes open from the fleeting dream that made close to no sense and was somehow still unpleasant. I felt no sense of rest, and an even greater feeling of frustration than the night before, but noticed one small warm peacefulness as I turned to see Maude sound asleep with her arms curled in close to her face. The night before she'd moved around a lot, probably to see if I was actually asleep. Once I had her fooled, I imagine it was only a matter of time before she drifted off like she was naturally supposed to.

I smirked as she lay there and embraced the quietness of the morning for another four seconds before the doorbell rang again, reminding me of the rest of the loud world.

The bell was followed by hard knocking. And the knocking was followed by a violent buzzing of my phone on the wood of the nightstand. I glanced at the caller ID and saw the name Cristine.

"Shit," I said in a hushed tone, before raising my voice to a commanding level. "Maude, get up, honey, now. You have to take a fast shower, come on, no hanging round in the hot water either."

Maude was an easy waker, she rose quietly before launching both her arms in the air for a long stretch and yawn. I paced through the hall and down the stairs. My upper lip twitched slightly before I rubbed and pinched at it with my hand. I answered the door in my pajama pants and white t-shirt, which is the first thing her wild beady eyes fixated on when she saw me.

"What the fuck, Nick?" Cristine said, the scowl on her face welcoming me like an old friend. "It's almost nine o'clock."

"We overslept." I replied.

'Yeah, I can see that."

"She's in the shower; she'll be ready in no time."

"Yeah we'll see, she loves to hang around in that hot water you know."

"Yeah Cris, I know all right," I rubbed my eyes and nose some more as I spoke.

"Stop," she commanded. "Don't do that, you're going to give yourself more lines on your cheeks."

I looked up from my palm and rolled my eyes. "Don't worry about my cheeks."

"You've got to go back on T.V. like 3 times this week, don't you?"

My voice strained as I quipped back, "Yeah well, they'll have makeup."

Cris bit her lip as her scowl toward me intensified. Her voice dropped as she said, "You don't have to treat me like a piece of shit. I'm just making sure you're okay. You look like you're on death row."

"Thanks," I responded passively before trailing off and turning toward the stairs. "Big, big help . . . MAUDE, HIGH SPEED, BUG."

I heard the shower turn off, meaning she was hanging out before I called to her. When I turned back to Cristine she stared back in anticipation.

"Are you going to let me in?"

"She's coming down," I responded while fidgeting in place. "Watch, she'll be here in like ten seconds."

Cris bit her lip again before shaking her head. "Wow."

"I'm just saying you're late enough because of me—"

"Whatever, Nick."

We stood across from one another at the doorway for ten long and silent seconds before I caved from the tension.

"You know what, no, come in," I said, frazzled, and motioned towards the kitchen. "I'm sorry I—"

"No." She cut me off and the said sternly, "I can't come in, I'm a piece of shit, remember?"

"MAUDE," I called again before turning back to Cris, "Will you stop? Just come in, it's fine."

Cris and I were launching into a full-blown argument before we were interrupted by two quick honks from a car horn as it pulled into my driveway. When he stepped out of the sedan, Martin stood just barely taller than its roof. His collared shirt was newly pressed, but it looked like he'd already begun to sweat through it as he hurried across the lawn carrying his folder tightly to his side. He'd forgotten to shut the car door behind him, and called to me from halfway across the lawn instead of waiting the extra ten feet.

"These goddamn numbers, Nick. Bryce is going to be on your ass for comments about them in this interview. You know he is. We need to spin it and look unworried, tell him you believe the silent majority will prefer to have their voices heard on Election Day and not in these polls they're running. When we're done with him we'll stop at the Italian-American Retiree meeting for some face time before we start on the last commercial. Hi, Cris."

Martin was out of breath by the time he reached us, but after a brief pause he spoke again. "And what did I tell you about looking at numbers late at night? When you texted me at one, I swear to God I nearly lost it on you."

"One?" Cris echoed as I shot Martin a look of contempt. "How late were you up last night? No wonder you couldn't get Maude ready this morning."

As if cued by her name, Maude bolted out from behind me and jumped from the third step on my porch to the ground, making a loud stomping sound as she did. Cris immediately scolded her, saying that she was itching to fall on her face if she kept doing that, but Maude took it in stride and asked her mother, "My hair's all wet, do you like it?"

"No! You're going to catch a cold, no I don't like it! And you need a sweatshirt." Maude's skinny arms were exposed, but I was relieved to see that she at least put on her jeans rather than her shorts. That would have gotten an even bigger rise out of Cris.

She then stood directly in front of Martin, looking up at him and reciting, "Washington, Adams, Jefferson, Madison, Monroe, Adams, Jackson, Van Buren, Harrison, Tyler, Polk."

"Adams twice?" Martin responded.

"Quincy Adams," Maude clarified.

"Atta-girl," he said and felt around in his pockets. "They're in the car, in the cup holder. Go ahead and get one . . . one!" Maude had already darted off towards the open driver's side door of the sedan before he finished. He looked at Cris and proudly proclaimed, "A new one every week, for a hard candy."

Cris just squinted at him and said, "She hasn't even had breakfast yet, Martin."

As he cursed himself under his breath I called out, "Maude save it for later, you have to have breakfast!"

"And I guess now I'll take her to breakfast, as if we aren't late enough."

As Cris walked away, Martin asked her in a hopeful tone, "Hey, uh, remember there's the City Hall Gala this weekend, lots of press . . . and stuff . . . we can count on you for it, right? We, uh, need to look as good as possible at it."

"I said I would come, didn't I?" Her eyes daggered into Martin for bringing up the event, but she completely avoided mine. She got in her car without another word to me.

"Bye, Dad!" Maude yelled as she ran from Martin's car to her mother's.

"Bye, honey, be good at school."

"Bye, kid," Martin called.

As Cris' engine turned over and she peeled away, Martin turned to me. My eyes were fixed on the car all the way down the block, and even still in its direction when it was out of sight. My nose flared at a sudden deep inhale that my body forced, as if to keep all the tired gears behind my face properly functioning.

"You all right?" Martin looked at me with concerned eyes, but I could also see the rest of his body shiver with impatience. It was more than likely he was on his second cup of coffee, and had a third mapped out in the near future.

"You got a cup for me in there?" I asked, motioning toward the car.

"Yeah," he responded with wide eyes. "You wanna go talk to Bryce in your fuckin' PJs?"

I looked down at myself and sighed before groaning to him, "Fuck, I'll be right out."

———————————

I stared out of the window of Martin's car while he drove nearly as fast as he talked. Everything was focused on the upcoming week. I started to zone out and nod off a little bit when he'd started to talk in circles about the latest poll and how he wasn't even sure if reflected the east side of town. Sure, it was the poorer side, he said, but I'd always carried in the low-income wards.

"Yo," he yelled, he must have caught me zoning out on him.

"What, what?" I responded. "Can you relax, you're giving me a fucking headache."

He looked back and forth from me to the road at least three times and said, "We gotta do something about your face. You look like a zombie."

"Yeah, well, you're no sight either," I grumbled under my breath.

"I'll talk to Theresa about getting you some more Ambien or something. Knock yourself out the next couple of nights without Maude. Then . . . well, after we get through that gala we're pretty much set— done with the hard part I mean. Well, that part . . ."

Martin was falling over his words now, unsure how to tread, and I couldn't blame him. When I thought ahead to the upcoming days, the gala, the election, there was an overarching sense of doom surrounding it all, doom that just waited patiently because it was inevitable. I shook my head before speaking to Martin in a deadpan voice, "So say we do pull of this gala, and she shows up and keeps up all of the appearances. Then the election comes, and hell, maybe I win and keep my fucking job, then she stands next to me in the victory speech, holds my arm with a smile for all the cameras . . . then what, man?"

I'd been staring straight ahead as I talked, but I could still feel Martin's eyes continuously turn to me in concern.

"Let's win the thing first," he said finally. "We'll take it from there, one step at a time . . . figure it out. Hell, maybe after some time, after the election and all the craziness dies down, maybe things will go back to normal between you two."

I didn't respond, but when the silence in the car seemed like it was worrying him I gave a half-hearted smile and nod.

I pressed my forehead against the window of Martin's car, and the cool glass soothed the aching and pulsing that had been building the entire night before. It was a crisp fall day out, and there were several clouds in the sky stretching on and on. Their supernatural-like presence made me feel smaller than before, but not in a way that made me nervous— the opposite actually. I closed my eyes imagining the clouds above and forgot my worries for a moment as I listened to my own thoughts. I seemed to cycle endlessly over one tiny obscure sentence.

"Clouds like milk and a spill like clouds like milk in a spill like clouds that—"

"Yo, Nick," I heard Martin say, and then nudge my shoulder. When I opened my eyes back up and turned to him he said, "We're here, you ready?"

My first reaction was to gaze around in astonishment. It seemed like only a moment ago we were on the road, and now we were all the way across town parked at City Hall.

"Yeah," I said with a deep breath.

"If Bryce isn't waiting in there already you can bet he'll be here in an hour or two," Martin extended the cup of coffee that I hadn't touched yet. "I told him you're booked after 12 so he's got to make it quick this time, the fucking sneaky bastard."

---

"Bryce, you fucking sneaky bastard, how are you?" Martin called as we walked through the lobby to my office.

Bryce laughed, brushing off Martin's crude humor. "It's a beautiful day, that's a start."

"A little cloudy," I said, leading the way through the door.

I'd guzzled more than half my coffee on the way upstairs, in preparation for our dialogue to come, remembering the worst-case scenario I'd played out in my head the night before. After his well-groomed small talk, Bryce delved straight into the tough questions that may have kept him as sleepless as me.

**Bryce:** Recent numbers have you down by a small margin; can you comment on these stats and whether your team is thinking about reevaluating their strategy?

**Me:** I saw the numbers that you're talking about, and I admit this year's been more interesting than I expected, but I'm not sure those numbers reflect the results you'll see next Tuesday.

**Bryce**: You have to admit though, Acosta-Campos is picking up particular steam in the current political climate. She speaks to several of the current movements like Me Too and Black Lives Matter.

**Me:** I'm right alongside her on both of those issues. My voting record shows that I've led on these issues during my time as mayor.

**Bryce:** Alongside her maybe, but some voters have voiced concerns about how vocal you are on them, and not to mention what seems to be a good amount of chumminess with Republicans in City Hall.

**Me:** Concerns? Chumminess?

**Bryce:** Their words, not mine.

**Me:**

**Bryce**: (Sips from metal water bottle)

I'd stopped dead mid-interview. I just sat still looking back at Bryce as if I were having a massive stroke. In reality though, I'd just lost any words to respond with.

"Our comment on that," Martin interjected. "Is that Nick has brought this city farther for ALL of the people who live here, like a mayor should, all while not compromising his democratic values, which you can see in his endorsements by local activists."

Bryce raised his eyebrows. "Throwing your hat in the race one of these days, big guy?"

"Off the record," Martin leaned in and gave his slightly crooked smile. "You can eat me, you skinny prick."

"I swear, Bryce," I finally spoke. "My daughter Maude acts just like you— the journalist archetype. She might even grill me more than you do sometimes."

Bryce smiled, "Maybe she'll be on my staff someday."

"You wish," Martin said.

The rest of the interview was uneventful, but I noticed Martin looming closer after his interjection, practically breathing down my neck. It was aggravating and made me want to turn around and smack him, but I kept my composure. Finally Bryce stood up. He stared down at his iPhone, saving the voice memo of our conversation and spoke nonchalantly.

"All right I think I'm good here. I'll see you gentlemen at the Gala this week, right?"

"Yep," I said, rubbing my heavy eyes.

"Your wife will be there, right?"

I felt a painful chill run through my body as I looked at Bryce. For the first time, I may have shared in the same scorn that Martin had for him. I picked apart the tone of his voice, and the sly smile on his face that seemed to stab at me. My jaw clenched before I forced it to move as I deliberately said, "Yeah."

"That's great, she's always a pleasure. See you two then," he'd hardly noticed my scorn as he beckoned, "Mr. Mayor," and left.

My eyes followed him all the way out of the door, but I stood still. It felt like an eternity, but was probably not even a moment, when Martin started his routine scolding.

"Yo," he called first and then motioned to the air as if he were writing a billboard word by word. "WE ARE PROGRESSIVE AND WE HAVE THE EXPERIENCE. How hard is it to stick to the message? What's going on with you? Do you need more coffee?"

Before I could launch into a shouting match with Martin my phone began to ring. At least, I thought it did based on the ringtone; however, once I felt my pocket, I realized it was empty. My neck twisted back and forth as I looked around the room, but Martin had also started digging into his pockets.

"That's me," he said. As he answered, I continued my own search nervously and angrily wondering how long I'd had an empty pocket.

Most people I knew tended to morph their voices on the phone into a slightly more pleasant version. Martin just got louder.

"Hello," he'd started before calling out more orders away from the phone. "TRACEY GET AN INTERN TO MAKE COFFEE. . . Hello. Yeah he's right here."

When I put Martin's phone to my ear, Cris was already talking.

"Are you ignoring me?" She asked.

"No I can't find my fucking . . ." I said, trailing off as I lifted a cushion from the chair I was sitting on.

"I've been calling you all morning. Did you leave it at home?"

I bit my tongue, literally, before saying "Shit."

"Are you all right?" Cris asked, somehow figuring out exactly the last question I wanted to hear at the moment, even after a full interview with Bryce.

"Yeah," I changed the subject quickly. "What's up, what did you need?"

"Nothing," she said sounding offended. I probably sounded harsher than I'd intended. "I'm just letting you know I'm going to bring Maude to my dad's house tonight."

"What, why?"

"I just need the night."

"What do you mean you need a night? What about last night?"

"Jesus Christ, Nick how many fucking nights do you get?"

"What do you need the night for?"

"You know what, forget it. Forget I called. I'll see you at the gala and—"

I thought I might crush Martin's phone in my hand as I spoke through my teeth. "Just stop, tell your dad to bring her over my house at 7. I'll take her tonight."

"What, so you can hold that over me? No."

"No, Jesus Christ. Just forget I said anything, Do whatever you want, Cris."

Martin was standing in front of me with an intense scowl and two steaming plastic cups in his hand. Earlier in the month he'd chewed out an intern for buying Styrofoam cups when we were supposed to be in support of passing a bill banning it from usage. He made her return the box and get plastic, which he held now. As I hung up and handed his phone back to him I said matter-of-factly, "We have to go back to my house, I forgot my phone."

"Fuck," He responded.

"I know," I sighed and lifted his keys out of his overstuffed pocket. I started to walk past him. "Save it, I'll leave now and be back before you know it."

He was behind me immediately, "Yeah I'm letting you drive my car the day I go on fuckin' weightwatchers."

He snatched the keys back. I grabbed the lanyard and

started a tug of war with him, which was difficult considering his low center of gravity. As we battled, his phone rang again distracting him and giving me the upper hand. I got the keys and started for the door, but when he shouted that it was once again Cris I stopped and reluctantly turned around. I stomped toward him like a child. As he handed the phone back to me, he snatched the keys and their flailing sharp edges scratched my palm. I winced in pain and jabbed him in the arm before putting my ear to the speaker.

"Maude wants to stay with you tonight," Cris said.

I closed my eyes. Despite the feeling of victory that warmed my chest I couldn't help but mouth a curse. After I hung up, Martin and I paused across from one another.

"What?" he asked. "What'd she want?"

# CHAPTER THREE
# DENTED

"Washington, Adams, Jefferson, Madison, Monroe, Quincy Adams, Jackson, Van Buren, Harrison, Polk, Tyler, Taylor," Maude said.

"What?" Martin responded in a disgusted expression, like he'd just smelled something rotten.

Maude's face grew sour too, at his response. And she tightened her posture before sternly proclaiming, "Washington, Adams, Jefferson, Madison, Monroe, Quincy Adams, Jackson, Van Buren, Harrison, Tyler, Polk, Taylor,"

"Ha!" he called. "Now that's more like it!"

"Maude," I interrupted sternly. Don't leave your homework on the table, you'll forget it tomorrow. Put it in your backpack."

Jack the Cat had made his way onto the table, and had begun to examine Maude's homework, first with his face and then with his paw. He was about to start gently scratching at it before Maude scooped him off the table and began to scold him. As she shooed him away and started to pack up her homework, Martin began to talk while discreetly facing away from me, hoping he could lower his voice to some frequency Maude wouldn't hear.

"You don't think Cris will bail on the gala, do you?" he said, more worried than he usually let on. "We really need her there."

"I don't know, man."

"Do you think you could talk to her? Just to be sure?" He was on his way out the door now, and suddenly seemed to want to take his words with him. "Or, no, I'll talk to her. Yeah,

I'll call her tomorrow or something. You just . . . just get some rest. Don't look at any numbers tonight."

"Are they supposed to release more already?"

"No. Just don't look at anything, for Christ's sake just go to sleep!"

"Easier said than done, chief."

I gave Martin a pronounced and sarcastic smile, one that conveyed just how little control he was in after I shut the door on him. He may have been the micromanager of my every breath during the day, but between 10 p.m. and 8 a.m. he may as well have been grasping at smoke. There was some relief to close the door on him, one less voice in the airspace around me. But I did have to admit that some part of me wished for his skills to extend beyond some magical level. I wished he could stick around and instruct me to go to sleep the same way he dictated my calendar or handed me flashcards of talking points for when I went on T.V. I could picture Martin bulldogging at some imaginary sandman, the way he did at Bryce whenever things weren't going our way. He'd say something along the lines of, "Two hours of sleep? That's what you're gonna come in here offering?! You must be using your own sand, because you're fucking dreaming, buddy!"

A soft meow below me drew my attention. Jack's green eyes were wide and meekly loving. I said aloud that he probably wanted me to feed him, and that I could at least manage to do that, if nothing else, for the rest of my miserable night. I immediately scrutinized myself for prematurely calling the night miserable. Some sense of superstition in me held on to a ridiculous belief of the power of visualization and actualization, that calling the night miserable would will it to be so. But I knew better at this point of my nights with Maude that my mood was about to take a spiraling plummet.

During my first term, when Cris and I still lived

together, there were days I could get home anytime between six and ten, depending on the type of constituents who had attended an open forum or panel. I could never quite nail down when Cris should cook and when she shouldn't. Then, some days, she would cook and I'd get caught up and have to text her not to set a place for me. No matter what, though, I always made it home before Maude was going to bed, so her nightly routine substituted for something more valuable. Most nights our family time happened at the bathroom sink rather than the dinner table. Maude would hum some song while scrubbing the minty paste over her jagged baby teeth, and few adult ones. She brushed for a ridiculously long amount of time, which I know is nothing to complain about, but she also wouldn't let Cris or I stop until she did.

The worst part lately had been that she stopped humming. The eerie silence accentuated what we were missing.

As we brushed I wondered about Cris, what she was doing and why she needed to be alone for the night. But I also wondered what was going on in her head. Whether she was thinking about Maude's and my night, driving herself crazy at the idea that I was letting Maude go wild, or if Cris somehow put us out of her mind entirely. This thought stabbed into me slowly, painfully. It would be one thing for Cris to forget about me for a night, that I could cope with. But the thought of her mentally putting aside Maude was practically unbearable. When I looked at Maude after thinking it, I wanted to grab ahold of her as tightly as I could and embrace her like never before in a hug that conveyed how purely precious she was.

Then I thought it would be best not to scare her by acting as strange as that. As nice as it may sound in theory, I bet it isn't every day that people's dads embrace them and refuse to let go. Though the ones that do probably have the right idea, and comparing myself to them made me ashamed. Standing in front of my own pale face in the mirror, I pictured myself as a dad who wasn't so concerned with faking routine.

"Good night," I said after putting her to bed. Just as I'd dreaded, her eyes looked up piercing and curious.

"Are you going to bed now too?" she asked.

"Soon, it's late."

Lying to my daughter was never pleasant, or easy. Never mind the fact that she seemed able to see through me like glass.

"It's not as late as last night when you were up on your phone."

"I had to check something important," I said with a grin.

"Do you have important things to check tonight?" she interrogated.

"Listen, don't worry about my bedtime, worry about yours. And that reminds me, no peanut butter and jelly fiascos tonight, okay?"

Maude's eyes widened and she sprang up out of bed tossing her covers off of her. She called out, "I didn't make any lunch again!"

I caught her by the armpits before she bolted into a sprint out the door. Placing her back in bed I said, "I'll make it, you just go to bed. Jack will help me."

"Jack the Cat," she corrected me.

"Jack the Cat," I mimicked, walking out. "Go to bed."

I closed her door resolutely and started down the hall, but shortly after to my own discontent, I heard the door open again. When I turned around Maude and already started speaking before I could give her any stern directions.

"I can't have peanut butter and jelly," she said. "All the jelly is in the trash."

"That's right . . ." I said with a sigh. "Well what do you want?"

"Chicken cutlets," she said resolutely, the way one does when they truly believe anything in the world is possible at any hour.

"You need to go to bed," I responded while shaking my head. "It's too late for chicken cutlets, and too late for whatever else that imagination of yours might cook up next."

"I know how to help cook cutlets, because Mom showed me, so I could—"

"Bed. I'll give you money to buy lunch tomorrow."

After putting her down for the second time, I retreated to my room, where I could already feel the air drifting in a challenging and almost insulting way, taunting at the sleep that I wouldn't be getting. And from the side of my eye I could see the little black rectangle placed on my dresser, plugged into the wall and faced down. I could picture its light initiating when I flipped it over to begin checking local articles, poll numbers and projections. At the same time as this urge, almost whispering in my ear, were Martin's words of caution demanding that I avoid any and all technology until the morning. In a way, it felt at first like an inspired remedy. I crawled under the heavy soft covers of my bed with some feeling of assurance that because I hadn't even taken a peek at anything to do with news or politics, that I'd soon be drifting carelessly to sleep.

What killed that assurance, not slowly or subtly, was the infuriating irony that while I could hardly stay awake in Martin's car that same morning, I was now as aggressively alert as I wished I could be after morning coffee.

In my frustration, I decided that I couldn't lay stewing in my own aggravation for as long as I had the night before. I didn't bother turning my pillow over to its cooler side, cycling my breathing or reaching for the seemingly useless bottle of rip-off spray. I stood up, my baggy pajama pants and tank top hanging off of me carelessly, and approached my phone. My hand had practically made contact before a sudden surge of will power made me pause . . . not a moment later my will was out of gas and I plucked my phone off its charger.

When the screen illuminated, a single text made itself boldly readable. It said in large lettering, *I KNOW YOU'RE GONNA WIND UP READING THIS. PUT IT DOWN. -M*

"Fu-uck," I breathed the curse softly and then obeyed against my annoyance, placing the phone face down again.

I turned back, glancing at my bed for a moment with its covers unmade, as if you could see my struggles in their wrinkles and folds. I felt my stomach and could suddenly imagine the small jar in my kitchen next to the toaster which contained individually wrapped pieces of chocolate.

I wasn't actually hungry, but as I walked down the hall I felt a nostalgic craving: that specific hunger to eat sweets late at night like I was a kid sneaking to the cookie jar. In my kitchen there was a tin that acted as the designated holder for sweet things, candy, cookies, whichever treat the season demanded could be found in it. When I reached for the tin there was a strange dissociation that came over me, as if it were completely out of place on the countertop. It was one of the few things that I took during the move, because I had the feeling I would have to bribe Maude a lot.

There was also a dent on the tin's side that I stared at with glazed eyes as I cracked open the lid and bit into a chocolate covered cookie.

Along with the crunch of the cookie on my teeth I could hear the muffled semblance of a conversation that was manifesting from my memory and into my ear. The recollection sounded like it was occurring underwater at first, but as I crashed onto the couch with the dented tin of cookies in my hand, it surfaced like a rising wave.

I held out the undented tin toward Cris across our marble-filled kitchen, which was spotless other than the small bundle of crumbs that had fallen from my bite of a cookie onto the countertop. She glared down at the group of crumbs with an exaggerated scorn as if she would incinerate them, had she the means to. I placed the tin down and slowly swept the crumbs into my hand, moving deliberately as though I were being watched by a wolf.

"Easy now," I mouthed. "I don't want any trouble."

"Fuck off," she replied jokingly while grabbing a cookie of her own. "I literally just cleaned."

When she bit, a new cluster of crumbs inevitably fell, and her eyes traveled down to follow them begrudgingly. She breathed in with a mouth half full and said, "Why do I even try."

"Relax," I replied. "Have another one."

In trying to be funny I'd moved too quickly, and the tin slipped from my hand and into the air. After a loud bang from the floor, my wife and I both looked over the countertop, dreading what we thought we'd find below.

"It . . . it didn't open," I said with my eyebrows raised.

". . . I can't believe it," she responded.

We lifted it and assessed the dent before placing it back on the table. It hit me quickly that I should go and check on Maude, to at least let her know what the sudden crash was. I flinched to start moving to her room, but Cris' hand stopped me.

"I'll go," she said and then scurried up the stairs. My eyes followed her before sinking back down to the countertop and the dented tin. I tried to fix it from the inside. Although a large portion of it snapped back into place with a metallic ping, some disfigurement was still showing.

When Cris got back she said that Maude had hardly noticed the bang, and that she was well on her way to falling *asleep. Trying to coax Maude into sleep hadn't become a common occurrence yet, so I wasn't nearly as relieved to hear Cris say that as I could have been. We continued some of our monotonous nightly routines and caught each other up on our days.*

*"Martin's already been gearing up for next year's race like some kind of doomsday prep-nut. He says that he doesn't trust any councilors in the city to not spring up some surprise campaign."*

*"Mmm," Cris replied faintly, washing a dish.*

*"I don't know why he's neurotic."*

*"But look what it's like for people to vote for a president, though, it's so—"*

*"This isn't for president of the United States, Cris, I'm a fuckin' mayor."*

*"—It's so intense, mean and split. People are really paying attention to every little thing now, and anything can explode at any moment."*

*"Yeah well, if people want to actually pay attention to my job nowadays they can be my guests."*

*"Of course you wouldn't mind the local celebrity status," Cris said sarcastically.*

*"At least among Dems," I responded in a dry tone. "But still, I can talk to anybody, pose for pictures, and they can look into my life all they want. I mean, at least I've got nothing to hide."*

*"No skeletons for you, huh?" she replied. "Listen to how pompous you sound."*

*"No skeletons. If you knew the feeling you'd enjoy it, too."*

*There was a momentary lull, where the only sound in the room came from the faucet of the sink which Cris seemed to forget was on.*

"What's that supposed to mean?"

"What?" My jaw clenched suddenly at the realization that I'd let myself go, and said something with an inflection I didn't consciously intend.

"'If I knew the feeling?'" she echoed. "Are you serious right now?"

She turned to me and stared with scorn, still ignoring the running sink behind her.

"Relax. That's not what I meant."

"You have to be kidding me, right? You know you are such a fucking politician the way you dig at me. You dig and then you sidestep like you're Ronald fucking Reagan."

"Turn off the sink."

"Yeah, now sidestep it, go ahead Nick."

I stared at her face coldly as I moved forward and reached past her head to turn off the water.

"You know what?" she said, seeming to quiet down slightly while still maintaining the same rage. "I may be a fuck up, but at least I'm straight-forward; at least I own my shit. I'm honest."

"Honest," I muttered back to her. "So now that's what we're using to label you."

"Fuck you."

"Real nice, Cris."

"Just another thing you can hold over me."

I told her I was finished talking to her and started to walk away. I felt a pressure begin to push out from the front of my skull, which felt as though it were growing triggered by Cris' mounting rage. She'd reached her threshold, the point at which she'd say whatever venomous thing she could think of.

"The only thing you're scared of is that it will come out in your fucking campaign. That no one will vote for a mayor who can't even look after his own wife."

*I turned around and started back toward her, breathing through a clenched jaw before saying, "Cris, shut the fuck up."*

*"But that's your political leverage on me, isn't it? That I fucked somebody else."*

*Something about the tone of Cris' voice, on top of the fact that she vocalized what often kept me lying awake at night pushed me over an edge that I didn't often acknowledge the existence of. I felt a sudden urge for violence, like an instinctual want for loud noises and slamming, and as I approached her my arm swiped at the countertop. Several things crashed onto the floor, including the cookie tin which was opened and further dented, as well as a few ceramic mugs and other glass decor. Her lip quivered as our eyes met an inch away from each other, but her face remained stiff and resolute. For a moment our entire home around us faded away, leaving only two people and the buffer of rage between them.*

*A sound from behind us made me turn around, and then totally erase all feelings of rage with a sudden sinking in my chest.*

"What are you doing?" Maude asked.

On the couch, I opened my eyes, which had begun to close without my realizing even though the tin of cookies was still in my hand. Maude stood in front of me in her pajamas. Rather than confused, she looked mostly vexed as if she had just uncovered a scandal that involved her taxpayer money.

"Are you eating all the cookies?" she asked.

"Uh . . ." I started before doing my best to side step. "What are you doing up? I thought I told you to go to bed like . . . a little while ago."

"I can't sleep," she said, putting her hands behind her back. Judging by her lack of persistence in her last question I assumed I hadn't dozed off on the couch for very long. She must have crept down the stairs shortly after my first cookie.

"You're way too young to not be able to sleep," I said while I stood up and placed the tin out of sight. "Trust me. You're up because you don't want to sleep, even though you should, and instead you're playing all-nighter like Mom and Spongebob."

When I'd stood up initially it was in preparation to lift and carry her back to bed, but there was something in the way she stood that made me hesitate. She had on a familiar posture and expression, drooped and wide eyed, to make me feel guilty. It was a daughter move that I'd encountered close to a hundred times before and yet still had no defense against.

"I haven't had chicken cutlets in a really, really long time," she started.

I did my best to shoot her down, "Maude, come on, it's late."

"But you and me are awake," she interrupted. "And we haven't cooked together since you, Mom and me all lived in the same house."

I gave a soft sigh while turning my head to look at the stove clock. It read 12:08. Maude stood like a statue with her hands still behind her back, not daring to smile even though I expected she wanted to. In that moment, the clock changed to say 12:09, which jolted me into a passing resilience. I breathed in deep and told Maude, "No," and that she had to go to bed. While she looked up at me I wondered if she knew that my resilience to her was about as strong as an old leaf. Either way, whether she knew or not, it crumbled like one.

# CHAPTER FOUR

# SPIN

I've never seen any sense in cooking without music. So even past midnight with Maude sitting on the kitchen counter, carefully trying to crack eggs and remove any pieces of shell that may have snuck through, Frank Sinatra's voice singing *I've Got the World on a String* could be heard throughout the house. I found it funny to think about how the same steady furniture that sat motionless each time I squirmed under my covers trying to get some sleep, were now in their same dark and motionless places but with echoes of big band swing music bouncing off of them.

When I was about to finish slicing the chicken breast into thin cutlets, I glanced over at Maude. Her hands were deep in a bowl of egg yolk, probably because she noticed a tiny flake of a shell in it.

"You washed your hands, right?" I said squinting.

She pulled her hand from the bowl and looked at it with wide eyes before replying, "Um . . . I did before"

"Right, I mean after you pet Jack when he came up."

"Um."

I told her it was all right and that she'd better go wash them now, as I poured out the bowl and rinsed it.

"I'm sorry," she called. "Can I still do the egg part?"

"Yes, I still have cutting . . . You know, for someone so hard on Christopher Thompson for his nose picking, you'd better be careful!"

"I would have remembered if I had my favorite soap, but it's at Mom's. It's from the doctor's office!"

I watched her wash her hands while she hummed a song under her breath. It was a strategy she used to keep track of the amount of time she spent rinsing, and by the end of it I'd looked past her toward the stove again. It was still before one o'clock, but I picked up my speed in cutting as if it were close to two. I tried to keep us at a steady pace so that I wouldn't feel immensely guilty about blatantly letting her break so many nightly rules and routines. While part of me held on to that anxiety, another part noticed that I felt completely awake for once, rather than caught between two states of consciousness.

Once the meat was cut and eggs were cracked, Maude and I set up an efficient work line. She took each cutlet, soaked it in egg yolk, and then coated it in bread crumbs. I handled the frying, because I didn't quite trust her near the stovetop yet. At first it seemed there would be no stack of cutlets to make her lunch with, because she and I were eating them almost as quickly as they were cooked. It was hard to blame us though, freshly hot cutlets were nearly irresistible, especially when I'd cut them so thin.

"Did your dad teach you how to make chicken cutlets?" Maude asked as she reached out to grab another.

"Actually, my mother did. Easy," I stopped her reach. "That one literally still has oil on it, you'll burn your fingers."

"Did you cook it with her, like we do?"

"I wasn't nearly as helpful as you, but I knew how she did it. Otherwise I just enjoyed it like a little glutton."

"What's a glutton?"

"What kind of cheese do you want on your sandwich?"

"Provolone,"

"All right well, we don't have that. American it is." I pulled the bag out of the refrigerator before turning back around to clean up our cooking area. I turned off the flame and placed the greasy pan in the sink, running water onto it and rinsing my hands one more time. I motioned for Maude to hand me the bowls that she'd been using.

As she handed the bowl over, Maude asked, "Can I help

do the dishes?"

"We have a dishwasher for that."

"Not for the big pan," she countered. "That won't fit."

"I'll do it tomorrow, c'mon it's time to go to bed, we had our fun."

A sudden knock on the door made Maude's eyes widen and me stop dead in my tracks. Although I already knew what time it was, I checked the clock again in disbelief. Every conclusion that my brain jumped to involved Cris at the door, and I may have been momentarily flat-lining while the horns surrounding Sinatra's voice rose to a triumphant blare. During that blaring the knocking continued, growing more frantic as the music crescendoed until finally a voice called out along with the knocking.

"Nick, goddamnit, open up right now!"

Maude's eyes were still wide, only now a smile formed along with her astonishment, as if a surprise appearance had been organized just for her.

"Martin!" she yelled, and then ran to open the door.

When Martin stepped into the house he already looked ready to murder me, but the sight of Maude in front of him added a whole extra layer of surprise and confusion to his already stress-stricken face.

He looked down at her with a furrowed brow and said in his exhaustedly loud voice, "Kid, what the heck are you doing up? You have school tomorrow."

"We're making chicken cutlets," she replied confidently.

Martin shot me a horrified look. He walked toward the countertop with Maude by his side to find the platter of what was left of the cutlets after making Maude's sandwich, and picking at them throughout. Even with the infuriated expression on his face he dug through the pile and picked out two of the biggest cutlets. He chomped into them enthusiastically and then spoke to Maude and me with half a mouthful.

"When I left before," he chewed. "I didn't realize you two were planning on having a Copacabana night. It sounds like an Italian wedding from the sidewalk."

"Maude was just going to bed," I announced while staring Martin down. "And I didn't realize you were keeping tabs out there, Martin. What, are you moonlighting as a private eye?"

"Goodnight Maude," Martin said while staring me down. "I just came from home because I had a feeling you were spending another night not resting for the campaign trail. Look at me with the lucky guess; I should go play lotto next."

Our stare-down was interrupted by Maude, who had apparently been brainstorming ideas for what to do next, since Martin arrived at the door. "Let's all stay up and play monopoly!"

"Absolutely not," I responded. "Go up to bed Maude, I'll pack up your lunch for the morning."

She replied pleading, "But we can make Martin's special iced tea, it'll help give us the energy!"

My eyebrows rose in surprise as he and I broke our stare down, but this time it was Martin to command Maude to go up to bed instead of me. When she was gone, he looked at me in total annoyance and asked, "What the hell are you doing? Do you know how much we need to do tomorrow? You know the gala is coming up and that's gonna be a nightmare in itself."

"Martin's special iced tea?" I said with my face scrunched.

"You put a little more mix in the cup and it makes it extra-sweet— look, that's not the fuckin' point. She'll knock out on her own eventually, she's a kid. YOU need to sleep. We are neck and neck with Acosta-Campos and you've been a walking zombie for weeks!"

Something in me snapped, maybe it was too late at night to field Martin's words of loving criticism, but either way I wasn't in the mood to be lectured.

"You think I'm doing this on purpose, you stout fuck?!" I reached down to grab his shoulders and seethed, "I cannot fucking sleep. I feel like I'm gonna die."

The music started to swell again and as I lifted the remote to press pause Martin called out, "Maybe because you're down here in your own personal crooner lounge!"

His voice lowered when the music stopped, "It's simple, Nick. You've been doing it your entire life, some years more than others. You go lie down on that oversized puffy cloud of a mattress up there, close your eyes, cuddle up to those silk pillow cases and let nature do the rest."

"Silk? What am I, the governor?"

"You'll never be at this fuckin' rate!"

"You don't get it," I said. "I can't just lie there with my eyes closed. Nothing happens. And my bed, it doesn't even feel like some cloud, it's like I'm lying on a fucking board of wood all night, until I finally have to get out of it in the morning, and then it's suddenly a bed again and every ounce of sleep I missed catches up with me. I just lay there every night, and I think in circles until the sun comes up."

"Well," Martin started, grabbing another cutlet off of the platter. "What do you think about?"

"What the fuck do you *think* I think about man?" I whispered and leaned across the counter and toward him, wondering what my eyes looked like. I'd started to avoid looking in too many mirrors unless I was about to go on T.V. after some makeup, because my face was starting to remind me of JFK's mid-missile crisis. It's like it's pulling itself apart, to spite me and every hour I spent making it stare at the ceiling.

"Hey Martin," Maude called in a soft voice from the

bottom of the steps. "What's a glutton?"

Martin's eyes widened as he looked down at the fourth half-eaten cutlet in his hand and then back up at Maude. His voice flew into defensive mode as he snapped back at her, "Wh — Get back to bed! You miniature demon, you're worse than your father."

When she begrudgingly turned around and went back up the stairs he returned to our conversation. Martin said, "Have you talked to Cris at all? About what you two are going to do going forward?"

"That's a bit hard considering we're making her keep the whole thing under wraps. Even if I knew what to say to her, I'd always be double checking to make sure she was on the same page when talking to the press, and ready to show up to any public appearances."

"The race is almost over," Martin replied assuringly. "What have we got left? The gala, election night? And then we're in the clear."

I thought about election night. I'll either be giving a victory or a concession speech to a crowd of people who voted for me and all the while Cris would be standing right behind me. To everyone in the crowd it would seem like an average married man stepping down from public office, or continuing in it. I tried to consider which one I preferred, which might lead to the best-case scenarios, but it was hard to predict. Staying in office likely meant more of the same: long hours and little-to-no chance of getting Cris back. And for the slightest moment, as Martin spoke with both hands laying against the island top, I thought about what losing would be like. I didn't consider how the concession speech would sound, or what it would be like to go back to teaching political science at the local university, I thought about the freedom a loss would bring and the enticing possibility of sleep. Then, almost against my will, I thought about the possibility of Cris coming back after a loss. This shook me, as if it were something on the cusp of dream and nightmare, either of which could come true at any moment. I thought about all the scorn I held for her in the pit of my stomach, and how it was surrounded by a childlike longing and missing. It was those two forces pushing and scratching one another inside my thoughts, hating and missing her, that made me wonder if I could let go of all of the things in my life that coincided with her leaving.

"You'll talk, you two," Martin broke in again, nonchalantly. "Election year, it's stressful on everybody. Hours get longer, headlines get weirder. It's a lot to handle, for anybody."

"You know you might be an optimist?" I said, rubbing my eyes. "Ever think of that?"

"Optimist my ass." He replied.

"Seems like you see the best in every situation we're in — at least you have for the past four years." I'd begun the feel like a statue that would never move from my own kitchen, but Martin broke that with a sudden smoothness in his next reply.

"It's called spin, Kid." He replied, and started to switch off the lights in the kitchen. "You've been in politics how long? You should know this by now. Spin."

"Okay, sensei." I still hadn't moved out of protest to him and his sudden all knowing demeanor.

"Nothing can pierce, nothing can stick," he said, covering the remaining cutlets in foil and placing them in the fridge. I wasn't even sure how he knew where the foil in my house was. "Everything can spin so that it turns around in a way that we win. *Everything*."

"You sound like a psychopath."

"Actually I'm a guy with close to twenty-eight years of experience in politics," he answered starkly. "But sure, if that's your way of putting it."

He continued, "How about you think, though. Have you recently heard of a successful politician taking shit from some headline that blew up one of their failures, or going on the news and saying they were 'sorry.'"

Slamming the fridge door shut, he looked at me intently and seemed to lean in as his voice grew lower but hoarser, "Spin, Nick. That's how we will win with what little time is left because no matter what comes at us from the meetings or the headlines or that sneaky fucking bastard Bryce, or Acosta-Campos, or Cris, or anyone and anything else that can try to jump up and bog us down, we are going to spin it and we are gonna come out on top."

I stared at Martin with wide eyes, half impressed at his passion, but half bewildered at his ridiculous fanaticism. I half-expected him to start foaming out of the mouth.

"Why didn't you ever run?" I asked offhand to break the strangely intense silence that had come between us.

"Too short," he answered quickly.

"Right," I droned back before saying, "Well, thanks for the little late night pep-talk, then. I guess you'll be heading out now to go prowl in the night around the city."

"Your ass," he replied. "I'm not going anywhere. What, so you can come back down in an hour and whip up a soufflé, and make us even later to start tomorrow? No! I'm sleeping on the couch."

I laughed. Although for a moment Martin's stubbornness seemed like intense resilience, I remembered he was often no more than a mule that could argue with me until the sun came up if his mind was made up.

"All right then." I said. "Enjoy the couch. See if you can spin what it does to your back by tomorrow morning. Goodnight."

I climbed up the stairs and slowed down as I approached Maude's door, but when I peaked in I saw that she was out-cold. Half of her body stuck out of the covers and her mouth drooped open. I imagined what it must have felt like for her, to fight off sleep so intensely but have it feel so inevitable. I pressed my eyes together intently trying to remember the last time a night went that way, and then I walked toward my room. When my head hit the pillow, I still heard Martin shuffling around the floor below me. I wondered what busy work he found to occupy himself with, while practically keeping guard at my door. He may have meant well, but every creak of my floor and scratch of movement that he made seemed to send a ripple in my hearing so that it not only kept me awake at that moment, but would for endless moments to come. I turned flat on my stomach *and buried my face in the pillow, groaning with my eyes closed.*

*"Stay up, I wanna talk," Cris whispered next to me.*

*"You just want to steal my sleep," I replied with my face in the pillow.*

*"Well, yeah!" she said, truthful and bubbly. "I like doing that, it's my favorite."*

*I turned onto my side toward her and grinned, "Yeah I know it's your favorite, which would be a lot weirder if I didn't think it was almost cute."*

*She smiled and kissed me, "Almost?"*

*"Don't push it, you strange, strange woman."*

*Suddenly she hopped up like an electric current had been shot through her. She jumped out of the covers and on top of me, trying to pin me down under both of her legs as she laughed and called out in hyper voice, "Give me the sleep! Now!!"*

After she pounced on me, my body jolted up. It was filled with a goofy playfulness that quickly dissipated when I realized I was alone.

*I slept*, was the first thought that offered some consolation after the comedown of the dream, but the clock unfortunately revealed that it hadn't been more than an hour.

My eyes were weightless, and I knew they would stay that way for the rest of the night. I reached out weakly to my nightstand for the spray bottle of lavender. After one spray of mist in the air I lay still for a second, then muttered a curse and tossed the bottle across the room. I heard it hit the side of my small aluminum trash bin and then bounce on to the floor. Then I put both hands over my face.

# CHAPTER FIVE
## GALA

The ballroom in City Hall was stylized in an old-fashioned way, so the walls were brown wood panel and a glass chandelier hung high above all the tables. I'd gone to at least two dozen event dinners in there over the years hosted by foundations, charity organizations and press conglomerates alike. I'd also hosted a few of my larger press conferences there, especially for high profile events like the transformer explosion at a power plant and string of assaults and murders by one gang that was surging into the mainstream. One of the more difficult conferences involved the missing child case of a small girl, which also happened during the height of combating the gang activity, but to every journalist and staff person's relief, the girl was found about 20 minutes into the conference. Martin had practically fallen over himself on the stage to whisper the news in my ear as I spoke. During the commotion of the conference breaking up, I snuck out a side door of the ballroom which led outside. I was leaning against the building and staring off the small hill it rested on toward the jumble of buildings and parked cars that made up one of the city's neighborhoods. I breathed a deep sigh for the near miss of a crisis and thought that if I still smoked, that would be the time to light a cigarette.

On the night of the City Hall Gala, the ballroom was bustling with more people than any of the press conferences, only in more formally festive attire. I arrived alone, after opting not to return home and simply getting dressed upstairs in the mayor's office. Practically everyone passing by me stopped for a greeting and a short conversation.

Two employees appeared to have already been a couple

drinks in as one asked in a high pitched voice, "Where is everybody, you're the lone wolf mayor right now!"

"On their way," I said back while forcibly raising the corners of my mouth. "I'm early."

I passed by people swiftly after making the obliged amount of banter, looking for the reserved table I was designated to go to, where I could stall for time. In the corner of the room's front stage was a technical setup of a keyboard and medium sized amplifier. Gary, the musician, nodded a friendly hello to me. We'd chatted with each other in the past during his breaks between sets. He was actually incredibly politically minded, like a punk rock musician, even though he played instrumental keyboard gigs at galas. He had a microphone to sing, but usually stuck to mellow instrumental piano tracks unless some special award or occasion called for a song, like "Happy Birthday." Luckily, mine was nowhere near.

I eyed the chairs around my table. There were four others besides mine, though one would definitely remain empty, as Martin rarely brought a date. I blinked slowly at the table, savoring the moment of peace when my eyes shut closed. As they opened, the chair next to me slid out. Someone had practically snuck to the table, and I tried to guess if it was Maude or Martin.

"Italian Jack Kennedy," said the person sitting down.

I chuckled and looked at him across the table and water glasses, "Councilman Vahey, good to see you."

"Thanks," he replied swiftly. "You look like shit."

I smiled again, only half forcing it, "Yeah, well, that's election year for you."

"Not for me!" he called in his old bombastic voice. "You should try being a Republican in this city; it's a lot easier on the joints. I mean, I don't have shit to worry about, I'm not heading up your way anytime soon!"

"I'm not sure I can finesse rich people enough," I replied sarcastically. "Careful Rog, all those retirees in your district might start checking out some former frat brother in the financial sector who wants to shake things up in public office."

"My fat-ass they will, I'll unplug their fuckin' breathing machines if they so much as think about it!"

We both laughed, but his was interrupted by a fit of coughing. He took a swig from a glass of water on the table. He continued after his throat was splashed, "Anyway, you're the one dealing with the up-and-comers. How old is this Acosta girl, twenty-two?"

"Twenty-eight," I corrected.

"Jesus," he replied. "You blues are starting younger and younger, like a college kid knows the first thing about leadership. You know where I was in my twenties? I was in uniform with a rifle, like it should be."

"Did they have women in the army back then, or were they still working on a cure for trench foot?" I quipped with a grin.

He gave a scratchy laugh before standing up. "I gotta get back to the table. You're a good one, Nicky, where's the wife, on her way?"

"Yeah, try not to leave too early."

As he walked off, I thought about drinking some water myself, but somehow felt oversaturated like it would come out my eyes. The music continued as the room got louder, and people found their way to the bar while waiters scattered across different corners and wall postings of the room. I'd been glancing up at the chandelier, which I must have selectively ignored in the past. The lights on it glimmered and refracted.

"Hi," Maude called in her best projecting voice.

I smiled, finally in a natural way, at the sound of her call. But once I turned, even that organic pleasantness died. I looked past Maude to see Martin striding alone.

"She called me," Martin anticipated my question. "Told me to drive the kid and she'd be right behind."

The moment was familiar, where whatever strange longing for her I felt turned to scorn at the emergence of a habit that drove me insane. I seethed, even as Maude wrapped herself around my arm. Martin seemed to capitalize on her initial calming assault by circling behind me and pushing down on my shoulder.

"Sit, relax," he commanded. "She'll be here."

I shook my head as my brain fired several different hateful scenarios of Cris, some of which involved cursing her out, others that attempted to figure out her intentions. I hesitated to sit down as Martin wrapped his jacket around the chair across from me. In an automatic tone, I said to him, "Vahey drank from your water."

His brow furrowed and he lifted the glass, saying, "That crotchety son of a . . . ."

"No cursing!" Maude snapped at him. "Mom said."

". . .gun," Martin finished with a breath. "I was gonna say gun."

"No you weren't," Maude replied.

"You weren't," I agreed while pinching the bone of my nose.

More guests filed in from outside, each seemed to resemble Cris in some way but she was nowhere to be seen. As time passed I felt myself growing both tense with nervousness and flushed with rage. I exhaled after what felt like an eternity when Maude tugged at my shirt sleeve.

"Can I go get a Shirley Temple?" she asked, pointing at the bar.

"Yeah," I replied with a big exhale. "I'll go with you, c'mon."

At the bar, one tan guy in his twenties stood in a black and white suit, using a soda gun to fill cocktails and popping bottle caps off a metal wedge in the bar. When Maude and I approached the bar he turned away from two people that were trying to signal him for drinks and smiled toward me.

"Evening, Mr. Mayor, what can I get for you?"

I grinned down the bar and said, "Actually, I need a minute. You can come back to me."

I turned around toward Maude, trying to seem unbothered as I spoke to her.

"So, what did Mom say, did she mention when she'd be here?" Before she could respond the bartender was back, even though more than five seconds couldn't have passed.

"It's so good to see you again, Mr. Mayor," he said.

"Uh, thanks," I said, bewildered. "I'll just take two Shirley Temples."

Someone walked up next to me and knocked on the bar, but when they spoke it was to me rather than to the eager bartender. Bryce.

"Interesting choice, I didn't know you had a sweet tooth," he said. His suit was blue and well-tailored. He also wore glasses, which was unusual for him, and I wondered if they had false lenses.

"Mom's here!" Maude called before I could say anything back to Bryce.

My tie seemed to tighten around my neck, and bend the muscles around my esophagus inward. But at least— contrary to all of the worst scenarios that sprouted in my mind— when I saw Cris at the entrance she looked like she was completely embracing our direction for the night. She waved hello to people with a smile and stopped to talk at those who jumped up and approached her. When she looked at me I was surprised to see the smile remain unhindered on her face and as she got closer, a new detail that I couldn't have prepared for revealed itself; she looked great. She'd curled her usually pin-straight hair and wore a black and white dress that I hadn't seen her in before. Over her shoulders was a white sweater, which she clutched at as she got closer, while scrunching her face in an exaggerated notion.

"It's so cold in here!" She said placing her hand on my shoulder.

"Cristine!" Bryce called out above the music and commotion of the room. "It's always a pleasure to see you, I hope you're well."

He stepped toward Cris suavely as he spoke and my eyes daggered at the slight outreach of his hand and its momentary contact to Cris' upper arm. My eyes followed him like a target in what felt like slow motion, only looking away to gauge Cris' reaction to him, but she remained neutral, too neutral for my jealousy to rise or fall relative to anything. Her mouth, coated in dark red lipstick stayed in a straight line as she returned greetings accordingly. Maude moved to her mother burying herself in the dress and sweater. As Cris embraced Maude into her side, my reality was checked and I snapped out of whatever primal rage towards Bryce had begun to ignite in my blood.

In her high and candid voice Maude asked, "Who are you?"

Bryce chuckled and kneeled down slightly to address her.

"I've heard a lot about you," he said. "Maude, isn't it? I'm Bryce, I'm a political journalist, so that means I write about your dad and other people like him for the news."

"I know what it means," Maude responded, scrunching her face.

"Trust me, you're no match," I said to Bryce, and

reached out to wrap my arm around Cris. Doing so felt painfully unnatural, especially because I could still remember a time when it was as natural as could be. Then the image of the three of us standing there together shined in a bitter way in my imagination, even before Bryce suggested he take a picture. His camera's flash had gone off twice already when Martin approached where we stood, his face already rosy with fluster and his shirt already stained with some kind of spill.

"Sorry Martin, I don't think you fit in with this photogenic bunch, even though you'd be second tallest for once" Bryce said.

Martin replied without hesitation, "Bite me, you prick."

*"Martin,"* Cris snapped at him and then motioned to Maude. "You're like a filter-less teenager, you know that?"

"Whoops . . . You look great Cristine," he said professionally before stepping to me and lowering his voice. Under his breath he muttered, "Look alive, Acosta-Campos is in the building."

I turned toward the ballroom entrance to see a tide of people shuffling and backing toward us at the bar. Looking past the edge of the crowd I saw the central figure, Iris Acosta-Campos. The crowd was orbiting around her like the sun and the hurl of questions and camera flashes were making her already wide eyes widen to such an extent that I thought they might extend beyond her face like a cartoon. Once the crowd got wind of my presence, they circumvented around my family, Martin and me, enclosing us into their orbit so that Acosta-Campos and I were directly across from each other like twin suns in a Star Wars movie.

"Go ahead and sit down," I whispered to Cris and Maude. "This will probably be a minute."

After motioning them away, I strode forward and extended my hand before Acosta did. Martin had been adamant that I stay faster than her on nearly every aspect of our meeting, especially the ones that might be caught on camera. I smiled first by a millisecond, but once she followed up it was clear that her teeth were far whiter than mine, and I assumed that her young face showed far less lines than my road-mapped late-thirties skin. At this I wondered how much of an advantage her makeup gave her, and by association thought of the 1960 debate where JFK trounced Nixon on TV by looks alone. Cameras had changed the rules of politics then, could skin-care and exfoliation be the stuff to do it next?

While all of this distracted me, Acosta beat me to the speaking-punch.

"Mr. Mayor, it's great to see you and your family tonight." She said, still shaking my hand. Something in both of our eyes signaled that we knew we were shaking too long, but neither of us wanted to let go first.

"Councilwoman, likewise . . ."

*Don't say she looks good,* Martin's voice rang in my head. *It'll spin you as a chauvinist. Don't comment that she went to your alma mater; it'll spin you as a crotchety old man. Stay civil tonight, look on-focus but not tunnel-visioned. Look rational, but not amenable to anyone around you.*

"You two haven't been in the same room for a time," Bryce said standing steadfast in his spot from earlier, in the center of all eyes. "I think everyone is waiting for a finish of that debate about affordable housing plans in the city."

She broke in quickly, "Well, it's not really a discussion that should be kept between me and the mayor alone, but with input from constituents who would be affected. So maybe, it's not something to talk about now, Bryce. We can all let Nick get to sit with his family."

*Don't back down from anything, but don't gun for her either— not at the gala at least.*

56

"I don't mind talking about it," I said. "As long as what the councilwoman and I say to one another is feasible and not just a race to offer more and more unrealistic proposals."

"I agree, unless of course complete inaction and gridlock is what you consider 'realistic,' Nick," she fired back.

*Show experience, but not elitism.*

"You have zeal to start with," I said quickly, and in a complimentary way that didn't give myself away to her too much, "But keep in mind nothing causes more gridlock than polarization. Look no further than Washington for evidence of that."

She smiled again at me before saying directly to Bryce, "I think he and I can easily agree we want as little similarity to Washington as possible."

Some of the people standing around us chuckled. Bryce's eyes lit up as whatever journalistic gears in his head turned rapidly. I wanted to go and sit down badly, but knew Martin would give me hell if I tried to walk away first. I caught a break when someone cut in front of Bryce and directed their attention straight at Acosta, asking if she'd heard the bartender call her name.

"I'm sorry, what's that?" She moved closer to them, and the edge of the bar, where an empty glass and a bottle of chardonnay stood alone on the polished wood.

"I said, can I offer you a glass of wine, Councilwoman? The house white." The bartender seemed as eager to serve her as he did me.

"No, thank you," she smiled. "Just water when you get a chance."

Bryce wound up being the first person to suggest breaking up the circle, and letting us get on with the gala. I'd turned to start walking away when he called my name again, and I thought my forebrain might burst if he tried to get some reactionary quote out of me in private now. I clenched my teeth in a half smile when I turned around, but relaxed with a breath when I saw he held up two glasses and said, "Those Shirley Temples you ordered!"

"I'll grab those from you," Martin stepped forward. He may have gone on to call Bryce a name when he took them, but I couldn't hear.

After catching up to me with the sodas, Martin turned to me and said, "I thought she'd go for the wine. I told that fuckin' bartender to pour it for her too, that way she was more inclined to take it. Now neither of you looks like the drinker."

I shrugged my shoulders, unsurprised at Martin's meddling at even the slightest detail.

Back at our table, Cris and Maude sat in front of the salads that had been put out early. Maude was sat up on her knees so she was at eye level with her mother.

"You will like it, trust me," Cris said, lifting a forkful of salad to her own mouth. "The dressing is just like the bottle kind we have at home."

"I don't like the tomatoes,"

"You don't like the big cut up ones, just the little cherry ones. That's okay, move those out of the way." As I sat down she turned and said, "How'd it go?"

"It was fine, uh, you know, the usual," I stuttered, the surrealness of the situation was starting to creep in on me, setting in my bones like numbness and pins and needles. "How are you?"

"Just hungry," she took another bite of salad. She was neutral, but not in a tranquilized way. She truly seemed to be in a routine, playing a part so well that the naturalness of it was uncanny.

"Thank you," I muttered. "Thanks for coming and— for just being here."

She turned and gave a smile, but it seemed sad, and rather than respond she just put her hand on the back of my neck and rubbed.

"Can I go to the bathroom?" Maude asked in a bored tone.

She was already halfway out of her chair before either Cris or I responded. The bathrooms were a close walk from our table, but I followed her with my eyes anyway as she maneuvered past tables and waiters. Somehow, I expected her to make a hard-right turn where she wasn't supposed to, and when she did I was out of my chair quickly, hoping not be followed by Martin like a shadow.

Surely enough, Martin's chair sprang outward one second after mine and he was behind me. I stopped him in his tracks and said, "Just keep Bryce off my ass while I get her."

I maneuvered through the same crowd that Maude had, only with a lot more trouble due to size. When I had her in my sight again I saw that she stood up pin straight, besides a slight and inquisitive tilt of her head, directly in front of my opponent: Iris Acosta-Campos. Iris was seated at her table with her campaign manager and others I didn't recognize. She'd pulled her chair out slightly when Maude approached, and was leaning forward with her elbows on her knees and hands together. They were at eye level. Iris was smiling again. She glanced quickly behind Maude to me twice, but then kept her eyes fixed forward as they spoke.

I looked around for Bryce, and saw that he had been successfully caught up by Martin before he could seize an opportunity for further action between Iris and me. I wondered what scornful words it took for Martin to stop him in his tracks, and hoped he wouldn't take things too far.

From where I stood I could hear Maude and Iris' conversation. I decided not to interrupt.

Curiously she asked, "You want to be the mayor?"

"That's right," Iris responded. "What do you want to be?"

Maude tilted her head to the other side, like she was analyzing my opponent for me, "I don't know, probably not the mayor though. I want to do something new."

"Well, you don't have to know right away," Iris ignored some bystanders who were gushing at the interaction and kept speaking, "I really didn't know until I got to college and even then it was hard to choose, especially because there are lots of people who will try and pick for you, and tell you where you belong."

"That sounds annoying," Maude answered.

"It is annoying! But unfortunately, that is the way some people are," Iris leaned in, "But let me tell you something. The truth is you can be anything, if you set your mind to it."

Maude furrowed her brow. Her gears started turning and she said, "But if you and my Dad both set your minds to being the mayor, you can't both be mayor, right? So that's only true sometimes."

Iris' smile gaped open slightly and her eyebrows rose as she glanced back at me. I just shrugged at her implying I was no help. She replied, "You know, you're right, Maude. Sometimes people don't get what they want, even when they try hard. I guess what I meant to say was: you can try anything and you can do your best at anything. And you may surprise yourself with what you can do."

"Yeah," Maude said low and unimpressed. "I kinda know that already. And I told it to my classmate, Christopher Thompson, when he said he wasn't gonna be able to pitch at kickball. He did pretty good when he tried it, too."

"That's a wonderful thing to do for somebody, Maude."

"I sprayed the ball with the hose after we played,

though. Because he picks his nose, it's really gross."

"*Okay*," I broke in quickly, placing my arms around Maude's shoulders to stop her from talking. "Iris is super busy tonight, bug. Let's let her be, the bathroom is that way."

I turned Maude in the proper direction before nodding a quick goodbye to Iris. I checked my watch once Maude ran to the bathroom, hoping that some hours had slipped by without me noticing, but somehow every stressor of the night occurred in under an hour. Near the bathrooms I did my best to subdue a vicious yawn while looking around in hopes that no one was watching. The yawn itself seemed to come back with a vengeance after I pushed it down, as it led to another one. At the third one I wondered if I'd ever stop, and imagined trying to speak to people as the mayor while perpetually yawning. Maude wound up being the one to catch me, as she suddenly appeared behind me, asking if I was tired. Instinctively I told her 'no,' and then grabbed her hand to guide her back to our table.

At our table a waitress in a black vest and tie took our dinner orders. If she hadn't been having a shitty night at work up to that point, she certainly started to after Martin spent 3 minutes grilling her about how her company wasn't serving any prime rib steak for the night. Cris and I took turns chastising and ordering him to relax. Maude ordered the salmon. When I asked if she was sure, she gave a resolute yes.

"Maude and I cooked salmon the other night," Cris said to assure me. "She loved it."

"She's a natural late-night chef! What time of night did you two get up to that?" Martin asked.

She looked at Martin and then at me, puzzled, "Dinner time, Martin . . . What do you mean what time?"

"I'll have the salmon as well!" I called while slapping the menu on the table, hoping to spear their conversation before it went any further.

Between ordering and receiving food, Martin, Cris and I attempted to make idle conversation, but I was constantly fielding visitors to our table. Each time someone approached with greetings or introductions, I noticed how the corners of Cris' mouth lifted and I tried to deduce how much force she was putting into appearing pleasantly obliged to each guest. She took their hands with a dutiful shake when they extended them, and she laughed loudly when they tried their hardest to be entertaining. It was only when our food arrived that people let off, and we could talk amongst ourselves, but it wasn't long before I wished the visitors would interrupt us again.

"Maude and I can find something to do the night before Election Day," Cris said, and then lowered her voice between bites. "It's a Sunday night, but I can still take her if you want."

My appetite started to subside, maybe because I personally started to buy into the illusion of stability that we were putting off. As a result, I wanted to regain some sort of control, and said, "It's all right, I can take her. Besides, Martin will probably be over that night to help out."

"Are you sure?"

Martin broke in, "We'll be fine, and you run off wherever."

"*Run off?*" Cris repeated.

"'Sneak off,' whatever."

Before Cris could respond the waitress appeared behind her and interrupted, "Can I take these out of your way?"

She stacked nearly empty dishes over her arms without any attempt at a polite smile, especially to Martin.

When the waitress walked away she seemed to leave a vacuum of tension that was festering in the silence left between Cris and Martin. As tired as I was, I could still see the invisible build up in the air between them. Martin had no idea that he'd pissed her off; he was speaking off the cuff as he usually did. In

Cris' eyes, however, she'd been insulted slyly by him and was preparing to start and all-out war against him for it. It wouldn't have been the first time the two of them tore into each other, but as I looked around I pictured the dramatic carnage that they had the potential of causing while people sat around enjoying their salmon and chicken francese.

A sudden outburst from Maude offered a solution.

"Martin," she said. "Can we play spit?"

"We just finished dinner, babe, they'll be back in a minute with cake." Cris interjected. "And we don't want to slam cards all over the table."

"I think it's okay if they play for five minutes," I called out trying not to sound desperate. I added, "You know, at those marble tables outside."

"Please Mom, the cake here is weird anyway."

Cris side-eyed Martin, who said calmly, "You know I love a game of spit."

He pulled a deck of cards from his jacket pocket, as if he'd been waiting all night for the game. Maude led the way to the city hall lobby just outside the ballroom doors while he followed and shuffled the cards. I breathed a sigh of relief through my nostrils and for a moment the full room felt quiet. The notes of the piano were sneaking through voices and they hung in the air in between Cris and me. She snuck her fork across to my plate to pick a piece of asparagus. I watched her bite it and give me an audacious grin, like she might be in trouble for stealing.

"You look lovely," I said, knowing that it would surprise her, which it seemed to.

She sighed and softly rolled her eyes with a smile. She repeated, "Lovely?"

"You heard me."

"You know that's my favorite word."

I shrugged my shoulders pretending to be ignorant, but it was clear that she saw right through me, so I laughed.

"You look handsome yourself, Mr. Mayor." She straightened my tie. "Just tired."

At that another yawn seemed to want to creep up, but I suppressed it and kept a casual face while she asked me, "How are you?"

"You know," I droned. "It's a crazy time . . . I'll get through it." Though I meant to ask how she was doing, something got crossed in the process of speaking and I asked, "How was your chicken?"

"Lovely," she said with a wink.

"Thank you for doing this."

"Don't," she said seeming to grow stoic. "You don't have to take things there. I'm here; can't we just leave it at that?"

"Do you want to be here?"

"Yes," she replied, in an annoyed voice. "Do you want me here?"

*"Yes"* I said, matching her tone.

"Okay, so let's just leave it at that then."

There was a long pause between us, interrupted only by some loud laughter by the Acosta-Campos table. It drew our attention in synchronization as we turned to look at her, and then returned to our respective silence.

"They're really eating her up aren't they?" Cris said. "She's so young."

"She's got the charisma of fresh eyes," I replied mundanely.

"Are you guys worried?"

"Always," I smiled and in a deadpan tone said, "But hey, if I lose I can dive into my forties and my midlife crisis head first."

She shook her head, "Or you could get some rest, finally. You wouldn't be on a crash course constantly. Or running around with Martin like a crazy person. You could get rid of those bags under your eyes too, I can't remember the last time I saw you with full color in your face."

As a sudden sting surged in my brain I scratched my face. I bit my lip and asked, "What, do you want me to lose?"

"I'm not saying I want you to lose, I'm saying things just might be simpler, and you seem like you could use that."

She was mimicking something in me, a voice that spoke in the back of my mind during the day which seemed to get louder every sleepless night. Somehow though, when she said it I found it easier to scrutinize. I said, "Maybe that's one way to spin losing, but I'm not quite there yet." She started to object, stating she wasn't trying to spin anything, but I cut her off saying, "I'm still in this so there's no good in counting me out."

I sprang out of my chair and made for the bar. The bartender's eyes lit up as he saw me approaching, and then to my side Cris had stood up and followed. While she spoke, all that ran through my head was how many eyes might be on us so I veered right to an empty section that gave some distance between us and the rest of the gala. Hung on the walls were decorative mirrors where our doubles stood as tensely as we did against the wall. I saw the bartender's shoulders drop in disappointment.

"Don't turn me into some bitchy anchor dragging you down. I'm not counting you out, I'm being realistic. Maude asks me why you don't sleep. She notices when you get quiet, and when you get short with me. This isn't just about being the fucking mayor, Nick; it's about the rest of your life."

I grabbed her wrist with my hand that was closest to the wall and while I kept an eye on the gala guests I seethed, "My life? And where the hell are you, Cris? How many times have you gone to the dermatologist lately?"

Her jaw tightened and I continued, "Seems like Maude is getting to know Dr. Uzan by this point, because you bring her around that sleazy fucking bastard."

I nearly hammered my fist into the wall as I muttered, "My daughter."

Even though I'd let go of her wrist she moved toward me with pure hatred in her eyes.

"I was honest with you. I told you I made the biggest mistake of my life, and you said you forgave me. You said we'd get through it for Maude, and then you ran for fucking mayor."

"Quiet down," I muttered, uselessly.

"Fucking politics, Nick, where every little thing has to look perfect, and every skeleton gets dragged out eventually. Where there's always some leverage or spinning. Do you think that's what I needed? What we needed?"

"Maybe not," I said, and my fist unclenched. Somewhere in all my tired where I least expected to find anything good, there was calm, but not the type that came from giving in.

"But I've wanted to be mayor from the moment you met me, that hasn't changed. Now even though I might lose this race, all I think about, especially when I lay up at night, is why you cheated. I stay up and I ask myself, was it something you thought you could do all along, or only when things got bad? Then, even when I finish running in circles and I tell myself it doesn't matter, because either way you still did it, I still can't sleep, because I can't stop fucking hating you for it and at the same time somehow still missing you like a little kid."

She looked at me silently. I noticed that her eyes appeared brand new, almost absent of every other thing that hung between us, unchanged from the days we dated, our wedding and the day we separated. It seemed unfair that they stayed so static when everything else was in flux, falling apart by the day.

"I've been seeing him again," she said. If she was angry before, the fire seemed to have gone out. She spoke now with cold indifference. "I think I should go. Everyone has seen me, so I think you're in the clear, but I can't do this anymore."

With nothing to respond to her with, I turned my head and glanced at our reflections, but the Cris and Nick in the mirrored ballroom offered no consolation. Her eyes were getting red and heavy, and he looked close to crumbling under an invisible weight on his suited shoulders.

I saw Martin and Maude approaching from the mirror, she still led the way and when she reached us she proclaimed, "I won three times in a row."

"She's a cheating terror," Martin muttered.

"I am not;" she snapped back. "If I have an ace I can pause the game and pick what I want it to be."

"Since when?!" he shouted. Once calming down, he looked at us in front of the mirror inquisitively. "You two all right?"

"Yes," Cris answered, though I still didn't speak. "We're going to get going, though. It's almost nine, so don't jump down my fucking throat Martin. You can tell that reporter you hate that I had to put Maude to bed."

"Language . . ." Martin said with dumbfounded eyes.

"C'mon, babe, you have school tomorrow," she said taking Maude's hand.

Cris had started to pull Maude away, but stopped when Maude softly stopped her. Cris let go of her and Maude walked up to me leaning against the wall and mirror. I looked down at her and faked a smile.

"Bye dad, love you," she said, and spun my fake smile into a real one.

When they left, Martin watched them with his hands on his hips. He turned back and forth between me and the gala and started his game planning, "All right, we can work with that. The hard part is over. Now we can work the rest of this night solo, give a few exit quotes. Tomorrow we'll focus on that online ad campaign. She's been fucking killing us on Instagram, that bullshit is wildfire with millennials."

In the middle of his rant I came off of the wall and made for the side door that I'd snuck out of in the past. He trailed behind me, still talking, before eventually saying, "You okay?"

"Nope," I responded resolutely. "Gimme a minute, Martin."

"You got it," he answered. It was in his nature to keep talking, but I heard him forcibly inhibit it.

The fall air on the side of city hall was brisk, and out to the gates several leaves had fallen throughout the day that would be gone by the time the grounds crew had lunch the next day. The streets of the neighborhood nearby were quiet, as they usually were even early in the night, besides the occasional car humming by. In that quiet hum of night I felt hyper aware of every sensation like the cold on my lips and breeze in my ear, yet I was totally oblivious to the person standing next to me, leaning against the building with their cell phone in their hand illuminating their face. They watched me, not trying to be silent, but not making enough noise to snap me out of a trance of thoughts that involved Cris' eyes, her words and the vague imagined face of a dermatologist I'd never met. Had I known they were there I may have gone back inside, and may not have vocally said the word, "Fuck."

"*Cierto*," she said. "Nights like these I wish could still smoke."

In a jolt, I turned and recognized the large eyes and dark hair of my opponent, Iris Acosta-Campos. She seemed mildly amused that she startled me and putting her phone away she said, "It figures we have the same hiding spot, doesn't it? And maybe five years ago you would have caught me with a cigarette out here."

Monotonously I said, "I thought your generation was more inclined to vaping."

She gave a short loud laugh, "A vaping politician?! I don't think that would go over well with anybody, besides maybe the vaping community."

"And they can't exactly carry a race," I said.

It was strange to stand quietly with her, absent of any reporters or camera shutters. Even a pause of a few seconds felt like an eternity, as if we were on a first date. I couldn't think of anything to say because there was no need to start a disputation with her or pick apart some claim she made. I wondered if I should lower my defenses, but I found it hard to gauge if she would do the same. As a dog barked in the distance I said, "You're popular in there, I see why you'd have to come hide."

"Not as popular as you," she replied. "Everyone wants to meet the mayor."

"Comes with the job," I said, and as the words left my mouth I felt strange to have said them.

After a long pause she said, "I bet it does . . . must feel good some of the time."

"Some days more than others."

"It doesn't look like you're having a good night for it . . . pardon me for saying."

"Is that how it looks?" I asked, keeping my voice steady and on guard. "Are you saying I just give off that vibe, transparently?"

"Well no," her tone changed to something unfamiliar. "But of everyone in there I probably have my eye on you the most."

"That's . . . undeniably true," I responded, understanding what it was like to shark after someone you were running against.

"Will you be okay?" she asked. The inexperience in her essence and in her eyes shone through. She genuinely meant well, and that goodwill made me chuckle from sheer surprise.

"I appreciate you asking, and meaning it." I said. "But it's not the time for a heart-to-heart between us, councilwoman."

Furrowing her brow, she said, "Do you really think I'd use it against you?"

"If you could figure out how to in three days, then you ought to," I said. "Especially if it would mean winning."

I felt neither warm nor victorious.

She murmured, "Seems too cold to be viable ... . having to spin everything, even your own life. What's it mean to live, then?"

"When you put it that way, it sounds like we should both quit. But I guess that's at the core of leadership, Iris," I offered. "No matter what, they picked us. The people we offered to lead decided we were the best for the job. So even if we don't get to pick what happens next in our lives we at least have to keep leading, for better or worse."

She looked at me intently and for a lull of time I expected her to interject, but instead she remained silent waiting for me continue. I softened my brow, letting go of the entire night for a moment, and said, "It feels good to win though," I smiled, "There's nothing like it."

I stretched my arms up into the cold air and failed to fight off a yawn. Then with a nod to Iris I opened the doors of the ballroom and went back inside to face the remainder of the night.

# CHAPTER SIX
# JACK

As the oven cracked open, a wave of heat touched all of the skin on my face and carried the smell of the garlic and parmesan that coated the chicken and potatoes on the sheet pan. Over the squeaking of the oven door and the clatter of me taking out the sheet in my mitt-covered hand, I could hear Martin speaking aloud while scrolling through his phone. The clock on the oven showed that it was still before eleven, which filled me with some relief. We were making excellent time.

"And how many young college guys do you think swung their vote because of Acosta-Campos' talent for batting those big eyes of hers," he lamented. "You know you can never really trust pretty people. Who knows when you've just got rose colored wool pulled over your eyes?"

"I don't think that's the expression," I said.

Maude returned from the bathroom with her hands held high in the air, outwardly indicating that she'd washed them. I nodded to her as Martin continued with, "Whatever, my point is you can bet your ass that no one ever had any problems trusting me in confidence."

"Do you and that lady have to see each other tomorrow after they decide who wins?" Maude asked while climbing onto an island chair.

"That's it," I said, placing out the tray of food. "No more talking about elections, votes or Iris Acosta-Campos for the rest of the night. And don't get too comfortable, Maude, after we set you up for lunch tomorrow it's time for bed."

She scrunched her nose, "No special iced tea for the night?"

"No special iced tea *ever!*" I called and glared at Martin. "You're going to rot out your teeth if you drink that."

Although projected numbers and Election Day schedules had been pulsing in my head for the past few hours, there was a brief moment while packing the meat and potatoes of Maude's lunch into Tupperware containers that things quieted down.

"Do I get to go vote with you and Martin, tomorrow?" Maude asked.

"School is still in session on Election Day," I said. "It's sad but true."

Running through my mind while Maude was lamenting about wanting to help fill out the ballot was the anticipation of seeing Cris in the morning. Since the gala we hadn't spoken to each other beyond the basic logistics of transporting Maude. More than once during both the day and night, I found myself wishing I could call out of every future interaction with her. Seeing her face again would surely come with a rush of emotions both unpleasant and pleasantly unpleasant, like the type of feeling that comes from feeling good with guilt.

The night of the gala I slept for three hours and ten minutes, which was the most I could remember making it in a long time. Every night after that was long and sleepless, and despite my best attempts, I still found it hard to make routine out of the seemingly endless hours. I didn't expect the night before elections to offer any respite. It was the type of evening that would have stolen my sleep from me even during my most worry-free years.

"Is it time for bed?" Maude asked and my eyebrows rose in shock. I'd been preparing to debate with her back and forth for at least another half hour before she considered going down, especially with Martin shuffling around the house full of unspent raw energy. He reminded me of a plump Energizer Bunny, only with speech patterns that were better fit to a Tarantino movie.

After saying goodnight to both Martin and me, Maude ascended the stairs and was followed by a scurrying Jack, who seemed himself to be slightly skittish for once. I thought I noticed a tiny trail being left by him on the wood of the stairs, but Martin demanded my attention before I could investigate further.

"The kid knows it's a big day tomorrow," he assured me. "That's why she's being a non-terror."

"Did you tell her that?"

"No, but she's a smart fuckin' kid for Christ's sake," he said, and despite his choice in words there was genuine admiration in his voice. "I mean, she's gonna have every president memorized by the time she's ten, I'm telling you."

"How long did it take you to learn them?" I asked in an uninterested way because I expected him to give a humble brag.

"It doesn't even matter, Nick. I learned them by rhythm — trial and error repetition— because my brother bet me a case of beer that I couldn't. Even a monkey can do that. The kid is different. She's learning them by meaning. I've asked her about each one and she can talk about what they did for the country, what happened while they were in office. She's turning herself into a little fuckin' encyclopedia of U.S. history, and she's not gonna stop there either. She's gifted. I wish I could say I'll live long enough to manage her campaign, but you've seen how I eat."

My eyes were wide and impressed, but still I corrected him, "She's not going into politics, I'm telling you."

"Yeah well, either way she'll be a whiz."

I leaned on my countertop and breathed in to a new warmness in my skull. Despite the long night ahead of me, hearing Martin's reports on Maude gave a sense of hope that was impossible to hinder, no matter any of my own circumstances. As the tightness released from the skin on my face, Martin struggled across from me with the cookie tin that I'd stared at in a daze several nights ago. He wasn't struggling to open it, as he had already eaten several cookies, rather he was pushing at it in an attempt to correct the stubborn little dents that were scattered across it.

"Trust me," I interjected. "It's no use. The little ones are a pain in the ass."

"You give in too easily," he replied without looking up. "That's why you can't get yourself to bed, ever. No persistence."

"I'm pretty sure trying super hard is exactly the opposite of what you need to do to sleep," I suggested, and took a carton of apple cider out of the fridge for some refreshment.

"Eh, what do you know?" he placed the tin down in aggravation before looking up. "What we should have been doing this whole time is getting you back on the ambient cycle. Seventeen doctors within a mile from here would have written a script for your drowsy ass."

"I told you that stuff hasn't worked for me in months,"

*"Dad!"*

The shrill scream made both Martin and I spring immediately into a run up the stairs. It was not a tone that

Maude's voice went into often, so the fear that filled her voice jumpstarted my pulse like a car engine.

We were up the stairs and through her door in a matter of seconds, and when my eyes darted around the room any semblance of calmness disappeared from my body. I noticed the red stains across Maude's white pajama sleeves and stutter-stepped to her in tunnel vision.

I was more awake than ever.

She looked at us with a distraught worry, the type I'd only seen when she walked in on Cris and me, the night our pastry tin was dented. When she spoke, it felt like I would receive whiplash from the transfer of my mind's worst case scenario back to reality. She sat on the floor next to her bed, with Jack the Cat lifted above her. In a quiet worry she told us, "Jack's paw is bleeding."

I tried both breathing to restore oxygen to my brain, and some careful examination of Jack, who was whining in pain.

"He's stuck pretty good," Martin said, out of breath at the door. "I'll get paper towels."

Maude's eyes were rounded in worry as she softly stroked his head, while I pressed the paper towels firmly against his paw. After a few minutes, Martin scoured his phone for advice on what to do next, and it seemed to be a consensus among search results that after close to half an hour of continuous bleeding we ought to bring him in to an animal hospital. There was no convincing Maude to stay home and go to sleep while we took care of things, as she was the first one to run to the hall closet for his carrying case and more paper towels to hold against him on the ride there. Martin drove in the urgent fashion that was normal for him, and this was one of the only recent situations where I considered it warranted.

In the passenger seat, I kept a close eye on Maude in the mirror, and the worry stricken on her face. I recalled the last time I visited an animal hospital, another late night only with Maude left behind. That night as Jack the Dog breathed heavily in my back seat, Maude stayed at home asleep and unaware. Tonight, however, there was no shielding her from fear or that stinging type of hurt that comes from watching the pain of one you love.

Maude was reluctant to let Jack go when the veterinarians ushered us into a brightly lit waiting room with off-white walls that showed a bumpy texture. The three of us were the only ones in the waiting room and didn't touch the old magazines scattered across the table, instead, each of us fidgeted uneasily in our seats. I sat in the middle of Maude and Martin, and of course began to feel drowsiness set in at the most inconvenient of times. I sat into my chair and knocked the back of my head against the wall harder than I intended, closing my eyes and holding in obscenities when I did so.

A vet came out to talk to us in quick fashion. I recognized her immediately as the same vet who delivered the news that Jack the Dog had fallen so intensely ill that there was little that could be done. Judging by her expression she recognized me as the mayor whose dog had passed away young, but she soon parted her lips and lifted her hands in an assuring gesture.

"Jack will be okay, he just got a nasty cut," she explained. "It looks like a shard of glass got wedged in his paw and got all pushed around when he tried to get it out."

"It's my fault," Maude said with her eyes drooped down

at the table. "I dropped the jelly on the ground when I tried to make a sandwich."

Before I could jump in and assure Maude that it was okay, the vet lowered herself and caught Maude's eyes. She had bright eyes and curly light hair. She spoke to Maude with a balance of kid-friendly tone and adult complexion that she appreciated. I watched Maude straighten back into her normal hopefulness as the vet said, "I'm sure Jack will forgive you if you apologize. Do you want to come and sit with him while I patch him up?"

Maude's head snapped to me, and I immediately gave a nod of approval. She sprang up to follow the vet, who smiled at me warmly before leading Maude back into Jack's room.

When the waiting room door closed Martin and I leaned back in our chairs, exhaling in relief and checking our phones in fear of any other unexpected events hurling toward us at the official start of Election Day, 12:00 A.M.

Martin blew air out of his mouth like he had a birthday cake in front of him. "Well," he said. "Think we should call up Cris, let her know about the fiasco now instead of waiting till tomorrow? Maybe she'll come on down here and join us."

I turned my head to him slowly and found that he was grinning as I expected him to be. He slapped my arms a couple times, I guessed in an attempt to lighten me up, and I gave an attempt at a laugh. I was still coming down from Maude's initial yell back at the house. As usual, things were tending to stick to me persistently, so reminders of Cris at the moment were as welcome as a heavy winter draft.

"Seriously though, when you see her tomorrow, see if she wants to stop by the hall for the results," Martin offered.

"The crazy season is almost over. Things will straighten out in a jiff, I bet. Especially with you standing up there accepting that elect again, mayoral as usual with that nice hair and slim figure of yours."

"Yeah, assuming we—"

"Shut up with that," he demanded quickly. "I don't even wanna hear anything like that; I'm telling you I'll slap the politician out of you."

"Bring it, Lee Atwater."

We shared a laugh before letting it die down again into the silent waiting room, both of us doing mental gymnastics in anticipation of the day to come. After a moment Martin spoke with unusual calmness, still looking forward as if he were in a nostalgic trance.

"It may work out better than you think, kid." He murmured. "Don't go giving up, I know you're not the type."

I looked at him in appreciation of his sincerity, but also with concern for his relentless hope.

"I had something serious once— she was like me, if you can imagine that," he chuckled. "We had a loud place, me and her, like a couple of bulls locking horns all the time. I'd known her since I was a kid, and you know I'm from the sticks so it's not like I've known a lot of people for that long except my parents. We almost married once or twice. Well, once was just us being drunk and crazy but I couldn't get the car to start anyway so we just stayed in and— well, we stayed in."

I watched nostalgia lift his eyes and his spirit and he continued, "She was the same way too, with this game. We were both on staff of the McGovern campaign back in '72, believe it or not. She was better at it, though. I spent too much time writing memos from the hotel bars with the other oddballs. She was one of the few that Hunter Thompson didn't get raging drunk with, because she took the damn job with some professionalism and not like a travelling fucking rock star, like I did. But she still screamed and shouted when we started to get our asses kicked."

He stopped, seeming to take a moment to reminisce to himself with brightness followed by neutral pondering.

"She couldn't have kids," he said suddenly. "We thought about settling down before we found out and . . . I don't know it made things harder. Things were different back then. She said we could adopt but that sort thing was . . . I didn't know about it."

After a long pause, it seemed he wanted to wrap things up, like he wished he'd never started. "Anyway, I kept saying I didn't know about it, and eventually we split. I saw her again in '94 . . . no . . . '98 . . . I thought, what a fuckin' idiot I was to let her go, you know? Even in '98, though, we must have gone to eight dinners in two months like a couple of kids in the dating game."

I nodded my head with scrunched eyes, amazed that in all our years together I'd never heard of Martin's former life in such a way.

"She died July of 2000," he said in a quick utterance. Then almost reflexively he added, "Never had to see 9/11, or those fuckin' Bush Jr. years. So at least there was that."

"Fuck, man," I spoke with my eyes fixed on his.

He turned and as if to offer me consolation for his loss he said, "It's all right, kid. We spent a lot of good years together. It's just a bitch that there were a lot more wasted in between . . .

and I never gave that adoption thing a chance . . . I don't know why. But that's what I wanna tell ya. What you don't do, you always regret that more than what you do."

I cupped my hands together and rubbed them for some friction in the otherwise frigid bright room. I eyed Martin, who sat next to me in a proud posture. His shoulders seem raised, and his head still nodded softly, reveling in the vulnerability that was just exposed. I sighed deeply, knowing that in order to say the words that were on my mind I would have to spit them out and deal with the aftermath after they were punctuated.

"Listen, uh . . ." I droned before trying hard to pick up the tone. "Back when we were still on city council . . . putting together a campaign and everything . . . Cris cheated on me with her dermatologist."

His head stop nodding and his neck bended toward me slowly. *"What?"* he seethed. *"Are you fucking kidding me?"*

I clenched my teeth together and shrugged my shoulders in a shiver as if I'd just told him I lost on a scratch-off.

Suddenly his right arm raised and slapped me in the chest, immediately followed by his left hand which was aimed for the back of my head. As his second hand made contact I shoved him so that his chair slid slightly and then wrestled with his arms so that he couldn't attempt another slap. The office assistant stationed at the check-in window peeked out in worry and confusion at the mini-slap fight between the mayor and his campaign manager in her waiting room.

"Well, why the hell didn't you tell me that?!" Martin called. "You said you guys hit a rough patch after Maude was born because of all the changes."

"We did, and then that happened."

"What the fuck!" He slammed his hands on the chair. The office assistant beckoned weakly from the window asking him to please quiet down, to which he called, "Sorry," and then whispered, "What the fuck?"

"Look," I said. "When she told me, we had a crisis between us, in the marriage, and tried to move forward, for Maude. But things progressively got worse through my first term, and now here we are."

"Here we've been playing some sick game we've never had to," Martin chimed in. "If you would have told me this was the deal we could have spun this differently. This is a whole other fucking . . . Jesus, what the fuck, Cris!"

I almost started to audibly curse and frighten the secretary myself, but instead leaned in, "I didn't wanna spin my fucking marriage, you sick fuck. It's hard enough wrapping my head around a divorce!"

"I mean spin like—" Martin scoffed. "Look, get over the terminology, I mean things are not how I've been treating them to be. I mean I just told you my life story like it paralleled your fuckin' . . . Jesus, what the fuck, Cris?"

I leaned back and shook my head, "I mean, I appreciated the story. You old sap, you."

"Go fuck yourself," He responded right back. We each leaned back into our chairs in the same way we did minutes before, sighing in unison and returning to mental gymnastics for the day to come. Strangely enough, moments after telling me to fuck myself, Martin said, "I'm sorry, kid. Issues aside, that's a shitty fucking shit thing to deal with. Not one you deserve."

"I know," I said, glancing at the table. "I don't know what I was thinking. She told me she fucked up, that she ruined everything and my first reaction was to try to make everything better. Fix things as if I made the mistake. But then that fades, that reactionary instinct, and the pain and the spite are still there. So no matter what, when she was still around there was always that hatred there. And then the past couple months have been . . . well, pretending is almost worse."

"I'm sorry," Martin said again, shaking his head. "I knew I was putting you through the ringer, but this is a whole different level than I thought."

I shrugged again. "I agreed to it . . . I think that instinct was still there, actually. It came back, the fixing one."

"Who else knows?" he asked with his brow furrowed.

I muttered a humming sound implying that I was thinking before gritting my teeth and saying, "Nope, just you, actually . . ."

He stared at me in an annoyed astonishment. I thought he might start with me again angrily but instead just patted my knee. The second pat hit exactly as the door opened and Maude came bouncing through holding Jack's carrying case with both arms. Her face showed relief and the vet's face behind her showed adoration for Maude as she showed us to the door of the case.

"They sewed up his paw so that it heals," she explained. "And they gave him medicine that made him super sleepy."

"You got any more?" Martin called.

On the drive back home I looked at Maude from the mirror of the front seat again. I was happy to see that her expression had relaxed from the good news about Jack the Cat, but also noticed something different in her while she gently stroked Jack's head with two fingers through the front of his case. There seemed a new type of disposition in her, not so much from active worry, but from the experience of seeing Jack hurt and being present as we moved in crisis for his sake. The chill of the sound of her scream was still lingering in the bones of my body, and I wondered if that terror and pain would ever again be replicated in her. While part of me hoped nothing could ever create such fear in her heart again, another more realistic essence in me knew that life was not so forgiving. I continued to look at her with this reality in mind, and lamented the fact that I could never completely protect her from darkness that lingered around us as we occupied the world.

When we stepped through the front door, Maude took Jack out of his carrying case and started up the stairs to her room. I told her I would be up in a moment after her to say goodnight.

"Goodnight, Martin," she said at the bottom of the stairs.

"Goodnight, kid," he responded. "Good job tonight. You were brave as a bull, next time we'll have some sweet iced tea to celebrate.

I shot Martin a glare as Maude walked up the stairs, but decided not to comment.

After I kicked off my shoes and stretched Martin asked, "So, are you staying down here for a while tonight? Wanna pour a glass of scotch?"

I thought for a moment and said, "No, I think I'll lay up there for a while. See what happens."

"Good," he said. "I think I'll have one myself, though.

Don't worry about setting an alarm, if you're out cold in the morning I'll get the kid ready, send her off with Cris . . ."

"That's not gonna happen," I said shaking my head. "But try to be cool tomorrow anyway. No sense in starting a war first thing in the morning."

"Yeah, yeah," he droned. "Hey, that vet was cute, wasn't she? Maybe you'd better bring Jack in for a check-up there soon . . . make sure he heals well."

"Let's make it through tomorrow first, coach."

As I ascended the stairs, I turned around to see Martin make for the bottle of scotch that he bought for me, but that I hadn't drank from. He poured a small glass and then made his way to the couch where he turned the TV on a low volume. As I looked at him I tried to picture the woman that he told me about, and what he could have been like as a young and ambitious kid, in love with her and politics.

Maude was already in bed when I opened her door. Jack was next to her, drowsily swaying from his medication and the bandaging on his paw. She stroked his head softly, and I joined her, until his green eyes closed in comfort and he drifted off.

"Martin's right," I said. "You were brave tonight, I'm proud of you."

"I got blood on my white PJs," she replied.

"We'll get them cleaned up, don't worry . . . or get some new ones."

After a pause, she spoke again, "I didn't want him to die like Jack the Dog. I know I was acting brave, like Martin said, but really I was scared. I felt like there was nothing I could do, and like it was all my fault."

I put my hand at the side of her arm and held her tight.

Then softly I said to her, "I know how you feel. I thought I swept up all that glass, but it turns out I missed a piece. And do you know what else? Martin said he thought he saw a shard by the corner of the fridge, but he wasn't sure so he ignored it."

Moving her covers completely over her I continued, "But none of that is important right now. Sometimes bad things will happen, and it will feel like there's nothing you can do."

"Then what do I do?"

With my eyes fixed on my daughter's I smiled and said, "You do what you can."

Jack lifted his head slightly, and then moved closer to Maude for warmth. Holding him, she looked to me and asked, "Are you going to sleep now?"

"Yeah," I said, fighting off the shake in my voice. "I'm going to try."

"Do you remember," she asked. "When me, you and mom went to visit pop-pop, and we were driving back over that long bridge with all the lights on it?"

"I remember," I started and then gave a squint. "Actually, I specifically remember us telling you to get some sleep. It was pretty late. You must have been being pretty quiet to fool her."

"I was looking out the window, at the lights."

"You just love staying up late, don't you?"

She nodded her head and then closed her eyes, nuzzling her face against Jack's fur. Then, with her eyes closed she said, "I miss when you and Mom lived together."

I felt my eyes well up in tears. And as I lifted my hand and stroked her hair I said, "Me too, honey, me too. But your Mom and I both love you so much. And we never ever want you to forget that."

I kissed her head and said goodnight, closing her door softly behind me.

While I walked down the hall to my door, all other thoughts were momentarily drowned out by a prolonged yawn that seemed to flood my entire brain until I reached the edge of my bed. My room was brisk like the fall air outside, due to a cracked window which I swiftly shut before climbing under the heavy covers and landing on the cool pillowcase. As the blood in my body settled to me lying on my side, my chest expanded with the flowing air in the room which I exhaled back out, sinking me deeper and deeper into the mattress underneath. Something was different. I felt lighter in my bed and though some of the moisture in my eyes from Maude's words was still there, our conversation seemed to leave the cranking gears of my head alone and drift out above me between my eyes and the ceiling. They hung there, still present but not pressing. For a moment a fleeting thought about apple cider trickled around the corners of my . . .

# EPILOGUE
# MAYOR

In the morning when my eyes opened and I lifted my ear off the pillow of my couch, I couldn't believe the number of surreal nightmares that had flown through my head throughout the night. It was like my brain was working overtime to flash me with unreal worst-case ideas about not only the election, but every single other freaky thing that could go on in my life. Still, putting their strangeness aside, I was grateful for the sleep. I would need it for the day to come, and as I climbed out of bed and stretched my arms, there were two scenarios that spun around me like an angel and devil chasing each other: winning and losing. My hands shook while the daylight broke through the bay window and I closed my eyes when I realized that I may have been sitting in the only silent moments that I would experience for the entire day.

Everything seemed to move both fast and slow, with a buzzing of staff members and reporters circling me throughout the day. My phone rang constantly, and when I wasn't on it talking, I was on it texting. Questions from the press were fielded on my way to and from the ballots, where I selected my own name, along with a list of other democrats running for different offices throughout the city. I saw my face on the news several times as a loop of coverage continuously played, making sure everyone in the city knew exactly who was going head to head, and where their votes would be counted toward. Sample ballots were presented on TV and online, and everywhere people were dawning "I Voted" stickers and buttons on their shirts, hats, glasses and any number of other locations both strange and comical.

Outside my polling place while I stood giving short interviews and pictures, I noticed for a second the beauty of the fall day. Brown leaves on the ground rustled by, and the trees shook from that breeze, as I breathed in the air to a brain that for the first time in a while, was generally free of pulsing and tired strain. I exhaled when a reporter asked earnestly, "Did you receive a voter pin in there?"

"Oh," I said, and dug into my pocket to pull out the "I Voted" pin. I clipped it onto my jacket and gave as big a smile as I could.

"Looks quite good on you," The same reporter spoke up from the crowd. I recognized him, and his flirtatious smile— Bryce. While my team and I started to walk away he trailed next to us. I wanted to snap at him, but did my best to maintain.

He got close, and some of my staff started to side-eye him anxiously. He said, "Tell me what's going through your head right now. Maybe something I can run with exclusively. Or, something off the record for now, and we can pick up for a real interview over dinner."

I blinked hard from irritation. As we neared our car he still lingered close by, as if he were about to climb in and come with us. I cocked my head to the side and echoed his words, "Off the record?"

I motioned to him and he grinned and leaned in with his ear protruding.

"You're a weasel," I whispered. "And you're not my type."

After climbing into the back seat of the car I rolled down the window. We'd started to drive away when I called, "I changed my mind you can put that on record!"

All day in passenger seats, guest chairs, and finally a bustling and crowded room full of TVs I greeted people, thanked them for their support, and did my best to remember to breathe as, one by one, polling places closed their doors and administered their final votes for counting. Despite anyone's best efforts, I was being pulled around the room with such zeal that I hardly had time to keep track of the incoming votes, or even the names that I was supposed to remember of some of my biggest supporters. When I apologized, all understood, and with enthusiasm wished me their best.

Finally I eyed the bar, and a certain corner of it where glasses of water were already lined up. I felt the dryness in my mouth singe as I started toward the glasses and their welcoming cool condensation. As I drew closer to the water, the volume of the crowd seemed to rise to a peak. While my eyes fixated, I felt a hand suddenly grasp around my arm, and yank me in front of a bright light and camera. With eyes wide, I looked around while the woman holding me spoke into a microphone.

"I can't let you go," the woman said. "She's right here, everybody. She's looking at herself on TV right now."

While she held me, I looked up to see my face projected on the largest screen in the room. Though the room was full, and extremely loud, my ears began to ring and drown out all noise. Both of my hands came to my mouth as I realized, *I won.*

"OH MY GOD," I exclaimed, at the words next to my picture: *Iris Acosta-Campos, projected winner, Mayor, City of Yonkers*

# ACKNOWLEDGEMENTS

To Chris and Cortney, this story started during our first brief stint as roommates and now it is all coming together as we enter our next phase (Or at least as I catch up to you) thank you for having your eyes on it from the start. To Kristen Kettles, your creative mind helped me through some of the deepest holes during this process. To Shelby Cundiff, beyond always being a creative sounding board, thank you for helping me unravel the mystery that was Maude's age. Alberto Contreras, you've helped me give this story a voice in more ways than one. Alyssa Vera, you consistently elevate my voice with yours. Joe Fries, I'm lucky you have such an eye for design and actual care to keep up with my work! Ann Marie Lawson, thank you for allowing me to take some semblance of a breather by combing through my extremely undercooked grammar. To Annie O'Sullivan, Bryan J. Mangam and Mike Deabold at Sighing in Unison, thank you for giving me my first platform above myself. Jess and Cody, you guys have a way of lifting me and my creative ability in ways that you may not realize, thank you for that. Michael Cronin, thank you for constantly trying to keep me business savvy. Finally to my entire family on Long Island (and Pennsylvania), I'm more than lucky to be surrounded by those as funny and undyingly supportive as all of you.

# Spin

Written by
B. John Gully

Executive Editors
Annie O'Sullivan
Bryan J. Mangam

Cover art by
Joe Fries

Published by SIU Press
a division of Sighing in Unison
sighinginunison.com